THE 3 SCORING CLUBS

ALSO BY JIM MCLEAN:

Golf Digest's *Ultimate Drill Book*

Golf Digest's *Book of Drills*

The Complete Idiot's Guide to Improving Your Short Game

Golf School

The Eight-Step Swing

The X-Factor Swing

THE 3 SCORING CLUBS

HOW TO RAISE THE LEVEL OF
YOUR DRIVING, PITCHING, AND PUTTING

Jim McLean

GOTHAM
BOOKS

GOTHAM BOOKS
Published by Penguin Group (USA) Inc.
375 Hudson Street, New York, New York 10014, U.S.A.
Penguin Group (Canada), 10 Alcorn Avenue, Toronto, Ontario, Canada M4V 3B2 (a division of
Pearson Penguin Canada Inc.); Penguin Books Ltd, 80 Strand, London WC2R 0RL, England; Penguin Ireland, 25 St Stephen's Green, Dublin 2, Ireland (a division of Penguin Books Ltd); Penguin
Group (Australia), 250 Camberwell Road, Camberwell, Victoria 3124, Australia (a division of Pearson Australia Group Pty Ltd); Penguin Books India Pvt Ltd, 11 Community Centre, Panchsheel
Park, New Delhi – 110 017, India; Penguin Group (NZ), cnr Airborne and Rosedale Roads, Albany,
Auckland 1310, New Zealand (a division of Pearson New Zealand Ltd); Penguin Books (South
Africa) (Pty) Ltd, 24 Sturdee Avenue, Rosebank, Johannesburg 2196, South Africa

Penguin Books Ltd, Registered Offices: 80 Strand, London WC2R 0RL, England

Published by Gotham Books, a division of Penguin Group (USA) Inc.

First printing, April 2005
10 9 8 7 6 5 4 3 2 1

Gotham Books and the skyscraper logo are trademarks of Penguin Group (USA) Inc.

LIBRARY OF CONGRESS CATALOGING-IN-PUBLICATION DATA

McLean, Jim, 1950–
    The 3 scoring clubs : how to raise the level of your driving, pitching, and putting /
by Jim McLean.
        p. cm.
    Includes bibliographical references and index.
    ISBN 1-592-40117-1 (alk. paper)
    1. Golf—Training.   2. Golf clubs (Sporting goods)   I. Title: Three scoring clubs.
II. Title.
GV979.T68M35 2005
796.352'3—dc22

                                                                    2004028691

Printed in the United States of America
Set in Garth Graphic with Rotis Sans Serif Bold
Designed by Sabrina Bowers

I dedicate this book to my amateur and pro students, who have all worked diligently to improve their driving, wedge play, and putting skills, and for that reason have taken their games to the next level.

CONTENTS

PART I: DRIVING LESSONS

Driving Instructions for Beginner Golfers

Driving Instructions for Mid-Level Golfers

Driving Instructions for Advanced Golfers

PART II: WEDGE WISDOM

Wedge Play for Beginner Golfers

Wedge-Play Instructions for Mid-Level Golfers

Wedge-Play Instructions for Advanced Golfers

PART III: PUTTING LESSONS

Putting Instructions for Beginner Golfers

Putting Instructions for Mid-Level Golfers

Putting Instructions for Advanced Golfers

FOREWORD

The thought and time Jim McLean has given to the game of golf goes unparalleled. He is on an endless mission to solve this game called golf—as we all are. I have personally discussed with him everyone's desire to dominate this game—if such a thing is even possible, since no one has ever been able to fully master even checkers yet. But he has the patience and passion to get his students to play at a level that they have the time to accomplish. He has helped people from all walks of life and all levels of the game. I don't know where he gets the energy.

The mission to get everyone better is his bottom line. While spending a week with Jim McLean at the Doral Golf Club we both explained to our classes that each person has a good swing in him. Let's start taking that swing now. Don't wait any longer to get good.

All the best,

Jack Burke, Jr.
Houston, Texas
February 2005

INTRODUCTION

In 1953, Herbert Warren Wind, the renowned writer for *The New Yorker* and *Sports Illustrated*, asked legendary golfer Ben Hogan to name the three most important scoring clubs.

Some years later, Wind asked teaching guru Harvey Penick the very same question.

Both times, the response was the same: *"Driver, Wedge, Putter."*

I know only too well the truth behind the words of Hogan and Penick, based on my long association with the game of golf.

Good scoring depends most on the golfer's ability to drive the ball accurately, hit on-target wedge shots, and possess a dependable putting game—in no specific order. So much so that, if a golfer can just improve the driver, wedge, and putter in a bag of fourteen clubs, he or she will lower their handicap dramatically enough to take their golf game to the next level. Specifically, the novice or high-handicap player, which I call a Beginner player; will move up and become an intermediate 10–20 handicap Mid-Level player, the Mid-Level player will progress to the low 1–9 handicap Advanced status; and the low 1–9 handicap Advanced player will be on his way to quickly evolving into a scratch golfer.

What sets *The 3 Scoring Clubs* apart from any other instruction book that I've written, or those that have been made available to golfers over the years, is its concentration on instruction for the three most important areas of the game. More importantly, rather than general instruction for all golfers, each part of the book is geared specifically to Beginner, Mid-Level, and Advanced right-handed players ("lefties" should simply reverse my instructions). Furthermore, each of the three parts of the book includes instructions on much more than technical driving, wedge-play, and putting tips. Based on my experience as a teacher and player, this book offers tips on equipment, shot-making, fault-fixing, on-course strategies, innovative practice, and how-to tips for thinking your way to lower scores. I've collected these tips for the benefit of each level of player looking to improve their scores and have more fun playing golf. I've also included anecdotes and secrets I've learned from legendary champions such as Ben Hogan, Jack Burke, Jr., Johnny Revolta, Ken Venturi, Gardner Dickinson, and Jack Nicklaus, and advice from top instructors like Claude Harmon, Butch Harmon, Carl Welty, and Harvey Penick, to better relay the instructional messages and expedite your learning process.

I believe *The 3 Scoring Clubs* is going to be your new guidebook to improving your golf game. So, let's go to the lesson tee and start with driving, move on to wedge play, and finish off with putting.

Good luck!

Jim McLean
Miami, Florida

THE 3 SCORING CLUBS

PART I

DRIVING LESSONS

When golf was first played some 600 years ago in Scotland, the driver was then called the play club. This is still a fitting name, because the driver is the club golfers depend on most to hit the ball down the fairway from the tee and put their soft ball in the best possible position to hit an attacking approach shot. If the drive is hit powerfully and true, the golfer is better able to play a shorter, more lofted club into the green. This is a big advantage and puts any golfer in an offensive position. Poor or weak drives always put you in a defensive position.

There's a reason why the power-driving game is the hot topic at 19th holes around the country, and why amateurs get charged up watching Tiger Woods, Vijay Singh, John Daly, Hank Kuehne, and Phil Mickelson launching the ball 300 yards in the air. Hitting the ball solidly off the tee and keeping drives in the short grass is a skill that separates the pro golfers who win major championships from pros who do not even qualify for these top events. Driving is also the difference for the top amateur golfers who shoot good scores so frequently. A good drive, especially on the opening hole, also raises a player's confidence and thus positively affects the rest of his or her game. Moreover, a player who drives the ball powerfully and accurately plays the game offensively rather than defensively.

In this part of *The 3 Scoring Clubs*, I will offer you an array of proven tips for improving your tee-shot skills—covering everything from how to pick the right driver to developing a technically sound power-swing to learning how to practice intelligently in order to maintain a good swinging action. Basic, intermediate, and advanced tips will be presented relative to Beginner, Mid-Level, and Advanced players, and I will even introduce unorthodox methods for helping golfers who have tried just about everything but failed in their quest to become powerful drivers of the golf ball.

Power is truly an asset, especially when dealing with today's 7,000-yard golf courses with long par-three, par-four, and par-five holes that require golfers to carry the ball over expansive water hazards and waste areas. With courses getting narrower, and often having deeper rough, every PGA Tour player is starting to pay more attention to hitting the ball accurately off the tee.

Hitting fairways is possibly more critical to scoring than ever before, for both pro and amateur players. Virtual unknown Ben Curtis won the 2003 British Open by hitting more fairways off the tee than any other golfer in the field, as did Todd Hamilton, the 2004 British Open champion. In this section, Beginner golfers will be taught the basics of my Eight-Step Swing, Mid-Level golfers how to improve swing tempo, timing, and rhythm, and Advanced players will be given the option to take the time to learn how to perfect the controlled power-fade—a shot that will allow them to work the ball back into the center of the fairway. So each type of golfer will be given a recipe for accuracy as well as power.

I've greatly enjoyed working with all types of golfers on hitting the driver, but I must admit that I continue to be astonished at the ideas they bring to the lesson tee. Golf is a sport in which opinions run wild. Every month there's some new magic move that appears as a magazine cover story that runs absolutely contradictory to last month's cover story. Almost always these ideas or teaching methods are based on opinion. Some books claim to have done research, yet teach a strict, one-way approach to swinging the golf club.

Golf teaching is often built on error-filled beliefs. It is no wonder so many people arrive at our golf schools totally confused while working with a detailed swing theory that will not work.

I've worked for thirty-five years with the best golf swing researcher on the planet, Carl Welty. Every idea I learn from top teachers, top players, biomechanics, books, and tapes is run by Carl first. Our rule is "we believe nothing." I will listen to any swing method or concept, but usually what I hear proves to be unreliable under the microscope of detailed research. My Eight-Step Swing System is not a method, but rather a comprehensive system of teaching the game. There is a huge difference between a method and a system: A method is tightly mandated, while systems are flexible.

DRIVING INSTRUCTIONS FOR BEGINNER GOLFERS

Chapter 1

THE RIGHT DRIVER FOR YOU

Buying a driver is a lot like shopping for a beautiful pair of shoes. The look must be good and the fit perfect to bring you a sense of comfort and confidence.

Your driver should be suited to your setup tendencies, natural strength, and physical size for it to work to your advantage. More specifically, it must match the demands of your own game. There are many variables that go into choosing the right driver, and the performance of the driver is top priority.

Let's discuss the clubhead of the driver. Currently, the United States Golf Association has placed a limit of 470 cubic centimeters on the size of the driver. The USGA has also placed a limit of .860 on the coefficient of restitution (COR). This means that eighty-six percent of the energy created in the swing can be transferred to the ball at impact. So when choosing a driver, make sure the club has the maximum allowable COR.

Today, there also is a growing trend that I highly recommend for making a driver fit a player's shot pattern. If your tendency is to slice the ball, a driver that features either a slightly "closed" face (i.e., angled inward from the toe of the face to the heel of the club) or weighting that limits the clubface from opening is an excellent option. Even the best players in the world use clubs with these types of adjustments. The typical pro is always toying with his driver, as you should. You can even do some experimenting with lead tape. If you hook the ball, place strips of tape on the toe of the club to alleviate your problem. If the slice is your nemesis, put lead tape on the heel of the club.

Another aspect of a proper driver is loft. The loft of a club relates to the angle of its face or hitting area. The driver has the least amount of loft of any club in a golfer's bag except the putter. If your swing speed is under eighty miles per hour and/or the trajectory of your tee shots flies too low, a driver with around 11

Only if your driver is suited to such vital variables as your natural setup position, physical strength, hand size, and swing- and shot-making tendencies, will you be able to consistently hit powerfully accurate drives that fly fast off the clubface at your designated target.

degrees of loft will help you hit longer shots that travel on a better trajectory. Those of you who generate clubhead speed over one hundred miles per hour and hit the ball high should consider a driver with 8.5 degrees of loft.

With a limit on the COR for drivers, the choice of shaft is very important. When picking a shaft, there are many important criteria to consider. These include the shaft weight, shaft kick-point, shaft material, shaft flex, and shaft length. For most players, pros and amateurs alike, the length and flex of the shaft are the two most important factors. Generally, the longer the shaft the more speed a player will be able to create; however, the club also becomes more difficult to hit. Many golfers who experiment with longer shafts hit more shots off-center and ones that fly left or right of their intended target.

For a beginner golfer, a driver that is forty-four inches long will be more than sufficient. Also, the flex of the shaft should match your swing speed. If your swing is under ninety-five miles per hour, you should choose a regular flex shaft. Players with speeds between 95 and 110 miles per hour should choose a stiff-flexed driver. If you swing faster than that, you will probably perform better with the driver if it is fitted with a super-stiff X-shaft.

When choosing a grip, there are several options. First, grips are either round or ribbed. A ribbed grip has a "reminder" bump running down the backside of the grip to help ensure the club is placed properly in your hands.

Grip size is critical, too. The size of your grip should match the size of your hands and the type of shot you want to hit. Players with bigger hands or who prefer to hit fade shots should go with a thicker grip. Players with smaller hands who prefer to hit a draw shot should go with a thin grip. The reason for this is that bigger grips reduce hand action and promote a fade, while thinner grips activate the hands and thus encourage a freer release action and, in turn, a right-to-left draw shot.

Grips are marked for your convenience; 58 stands for regular size; 60 or "X-core" is undersized; 56 is slightly larger. To find those numbers, flip up the lower end of the grip and you'll see a small number inside.

Take your club-fitting selections seriously, because you want a driver specifically suited to you and your game. Hitting a good drive down the center of the fairway allows you the opportunity to play each hole offensively. Long, straight drives are a huge advantage. Any better player will tell you how crucial driving can be. So take all the time you need in choosing the driver just for your golf swing. Then improve your driving fundamentals and trust your swing.

Chapter 2

TECHNICAL TERMS EXPLAINED SIMPLY

The longer you play this great game, the more into it you will get. Even the way you talk changes. Just play with a threesome of advanced golfers and you'll know what I'm talking about—if you don't already.

In case you get paired with better players who speak the language of the links, or "golfspeak," let me enhance your vocabulary. That way, you'll understand the words and phrases uttered by more advanced golfers and be able to join in the conversation. Furthermore, you'll have a better understanding of the swing and what I'm talking about in the upcoming chapters.

DEFINITIONS

Across-the-Line: The club's shaft points right of the target line when the player reaches the top of the swing.

The *across-the-line* position.

Address: The golfer's starting position or setup.

At the Top: The end point of the backswing.

Banana Ball: A slice shot that curves from left to right, forming the shape of a banana.

Carry: How far the ball flies in the air.

Closed Stance: At address, the right foot is farther from the target line than the left foot.

Here, I take a *closed stance* at address.

Clubface: The grooved hitting portion of the clubhead.

Clubhead: The part of the driver that features the clubface, heel, and toe. The toe is the end of the clubhead farthest from the golfer. The heel is the end of the clubhead closest to the golfer.

Clubhead Speed: The speed of the club during the swing.

Draw: A controlled shot that flies slightly from right to left.

Duck Hook: A shot that darts left, then turns even farther left, before landing with exaggerated topspin.

Fade: A controlled shot that flies slightly from left to right.

Flat Spot: The low point in the swing, prior to impact and after impact, where the clubhead sweeps along the ground.

Flat Swing: A rounded, less upright swing. The club is swung around the body at a low angle.

Impact: The point at which the ball is struck with the clubface.

Inside: The area on the golfer's side of the target line.

Inside-Out: Swinging the club from inside the target line on the backswing and out at the ball on the downswing.

The streamlined look of the clubhead, moving low to the ground prior to and after impact, is the *flat spot*.

Laid-Off: The clubhead points well left of the target when the player reaches the top of the swing.

The *laid-off* position.

Leading Edge: The very front edge at the bottom of the clubhead, used for aiming.

Lie: The angle that the clubshaft makes with the ground when the club is soled in its natural position.

Loft: The degree of pitch built into the clubhead, designed to lift the ball into the air.

Open Stance: At address, the left foot is farther from the target line than the right foot.

Here I take an *open stance* at address.

Outside: The area outside the target line farthest from the golfer.

Outside-In: Swinging the club outside the target line on the backswing and then across it coming down.

Parallel Position: The point at the top of the backswing when the clubshaft is parallel to the target line. Also, halfway back in the backswing and halfway through in the forward swing.

The classic *parallel* position at the top of the backswing.

Path: The line on which the club travels: straight back along the target line, inside the target line, or outside the target line.

Plane: The angle that the club swings on. The plane of the swing is actually similar to the roofline of a house.

Here the arms, hands, and club have dropped into the ideal hitting *slot*.

Slot: The perfect downswing position to deliver the club into the ball.

Square Alignment: At address, the player's body is parallel to the target line and the club is square to the target.

Square Clubface: At address, the club is set perpendicular to the target line and the clubface is aimed at an area of fairway on a tee shot, an area of green on a pitch, or the hole or the aim-point on a putt.

Square Stance: At address, the player's feet are parallel to the target line.

Sweet Spot: The center portion of the clubface.

Takeaway: The first part of the swing, when the club travels back away from the ball, low to the ground, for approximately two feet.

This early move back, or *takeaway*, often dictates the tempo, timing, and rhythm of your swing.

Target Line: An imaginary line running from the ball to the target.

Tempo: The speed or pace of the swing.

Timing: The coordinated movement of the golf club with the movement of the body.

Upright Swing: The arms swing the club up on a steep angle on the backswing and downswing.

Waggle: The preliminary movement of the club prior to the swing.

Here, I *waggle* the club like former British Open champion Justin Leonard.

FAMILIAR PHRASES/TRANSLATIONS

Golfer: "I took it inside."

Translation: I swung the club back well inside the target line, on too flat or too rounded a plane or angle.

Here's a down-the-line picture of taking the club outside the target line.

Golfer: "I took it outside."
Translation: I took the club back well outside the target line.

Golfer: "I didn't turn."
Translation: I failed to coil my shoulders and hips in a clockwise direction on the backswing.

Golfer: "I came over the top."

Translation: I jutted my right shoulder outward, then pulled the club down across the target line and the ball.

The diabolical, shot-destroying over-the-top move at the start of the downswing.

Golfer: "I didn't stay down."

Translation: I failed to maintain the flex in my knees, or I changed my spine angle, on the downswing.

Golfer: "I had no flat spot."

Translation: I failed to keep the club moving low to the ground just before and just after impact.

Chapter 3

SETTING UP TO DRIVE

The majority of high-handicap beginner golfers have no clue about the importance of the address position, which is why I see such a variety of setup styles at my golf schools. Unfortunately, because these golfers set up incorrectly, they often hit wayward shots. Don't make the same mistake, or you'll remain a poor player for your entire golfing life. Do not underestimate the importance of the setup.

I love the quote by Jack Nicklaus that golf is "fifty percent setup." The setup, to a large degree, predetermines not only the path that the club travels along and the plane or angle on which you swing the club, but also the quality of your motion at every stage of the action—and, ultimately, the quality of the shot you hit. So to reach your goal of becoming a better golfer, or to even reach pro status, you must first learn the following regarding grip, stance, ball position, posture, and body and clubface alignment. (See the color insert in the Driving Lessons segment for the Beginner Player.)

GRIP

In a power swing, the golf club moves in harmony with the body. Because the hands are the only parts of your body that are directly connected to the club, the way you grip is crucial to the swing you make and the outcome of the shots you hit.

There are three main ways to hold the club: with an overlap, an interlocking, or a ten-finger grip. Some great players in the past have used such unconventional grips as the cross-handed grip or the reverse-overlap, but these are exceptions to the rule.

In the *overlap* style of grip used by the majority of tour players (sometimes called the "Vardon" grip after Harry Vardon, the legendary golfer who popularized it), the hands are wedded together with the little finger of the right hand resting atop, or overlapping, the index finger of the left hand.

The grip used by Jack Nicklaus, Tiger Woods, John Daly, Tom Kite, Bruce Lietzke, Tom Kite, and Nancy Lopez is called the *interlocking* grip, which is normally recommended for players with small hands. This grip is similar to the overlap grip in that the little finger of the right hand is the finger that meshes the right hand with the left. However, instead of the right pinky overlapping the left index finger, it interlocks with the index finger of the left hand.

The third type of grip is known as the *ten-finger* or *baseball* grip. In this style, no wedding or overlapping of the hands is involved at all. The entire right hand simply rests on the club's handle directly beneath the left, as though you were holding a baseball bat.

The *overlap* grip.

The *interlock* grip.

The *ten-finger* or *baseball* grip.

The ten-finger grip is employed by a very small percentage of professional and amateur golfers. Many golf teachers strongly discourage students from using this grip because they believe that if the hands are not in some way connected, they will tend to work against each other rather than operate as a coordinated unit, particularly in the impact zone. Having experimented with the ten-finger grip as a youngster learning the game, I tend to agree. Nevertheless, some great golf has definitely been played with this grip. For example, Art Wall, a former Masters champion, and Bob Rosburg, a former PGA champion, both used the ten-finger grip. Other top-class players who use this grip include Beth Daniel, a major championship winner on the LPGA Tour and a Hall of Fame member; Bob Estes, a fine PGA Tour player; and Dave Barr, one of Canada's all-time best golfers. So I'm not going to rule it out.

As you can see, each style of grip is distinctive. However, there remain a few characteristics that hold true to form.

The first of these principles is the way you wrap your hands around the grip-end of the golf club. The grip should lie diagonally across the base of your fingers and partially in the palm of your left hand, while resting predominantly in the fingers of your right hand.

Getting the hands to work as a unified team is my goal, and it should also be yours every time you grip the club. To accomplish this, take great care to build a cohesive unified grip that molds your hands into a single unit. The palms will virtually face each other. In other words, after gripping, if you were to open your hands, extend your fingers and let go of the club, your palms would align.

Another checkpoint I recommend using to confirm that your hands are gripping the club properly is the position of the two "V"s formed by the thumb and forefinger of each hand. Once you take your setup, which I'll explain shortly, look down and confirm that the Vs are in an acceptable range—that is, pointing between your chin and right shoulder. You will tend to open the clubface more with the Vs pointed up to the chin, and close the clubface with the Vs pointed toward the shoulder.

The configuration of your grip is very important, but grip pressure is perhaps even more critical. The right amount of pressure is the final principle you must adhere to. As a general rule, you should grip a little more firmly with the last three fingers of your left hand and with the middle two fingers of your right.

These are two of the three vital pressure points of any good grip. To be certain that you're not gripping too firmly, or too tightly, during practice or a casual round, ask a friend or playing partner to pull the club from your grasp. If both of you feel just a slight resistance, your grip pressure is likely good. This means that you're holding the club lightly enough to feel the clubhead and firmly enough to withstand the force of impact. (When competing in an official tournament, when you are not permitted by the rules to seek the advice of a fellow player, look for shot-making signs to detect a faulty grip. Weak shots can often be traced to an extra-firm, tense grip, while wayward shots flying left or right of the target may indicate a loose grip.)

When testing your grip pressure at home or on the driving range, use the 1–10 scale that I invented, which is designed to get golfers away from the various abstract thoughts put forth by some teachers: "Hold the club with the same pressure you use to squeeze a tube of toothpaste." Super light is 1 or 2. Super tight is 9 or 10. Your midway pressure level is 5. Practice all ten levels of pressure by holding your club in front of your eyes. I have my students close their eyes as they practice the grip scale to further emphasize the feel in their fingers.

STANCE, POSTURE, BODY ALIGNMENT

The angles you set at address are crucial to accurate driving. You simply want to put yourself in the best possible position to deliver the clubhead squarely into the ball at maximum speed.

When teaching most golfers, but certainly beginner-level players, to drive a golf ball, I advocate a square stance. In order to encourage this position, I tell students to imagine standing perpendicular to a set of train tracks, with the outside rail running directly from the ball to the target, and the inside rail (the line across your toes) running to a spot a fraction to the left of your target. You should also use this visual image before physically rehearsing the proper square stance in practice.

The *square setup*, from the front view.

When practicing, get in the habit of starting your setup routine from a position several steps behind the ball. As you walk around the side of the ball, first place the clubhead directly behind the ball. Your feet will be very close together with the back foot closer to the ball. From this position, you can easily look down your target line and balance your body. There is no rush at this stage. You can take extra seconds to adjust yourself. You are not "on the clock." The preshot clock actually starts when you position your feet and it is important to make this next move precise. The next move is placing your left foot into the correct position. It will be a small step forward, placing the golf ball just inside the left heel. In this way, you can control ball position every time with your ball off the instep, one inch behind it, two inches behind it, etc. Then you can drop your right foot into a position parallel to the target line and you're ready to go.

Whereas the majority of teachers advocate a shoulder-width stance for driving, I like beginners and high-handicap weekend players to experiment between a stance that's narrower than shoulder-width and one that's wider. If you are "swing locked," the narrow stance, with each foot turned out approximately ten degrees will set you loose. It's easier to turn your hips from the narrow stance, although for the advanced player I advocate a wide stance. The reason: It promotes more resistance in the lower body and more potential for torque. The game's best drivers, most notably eight-time major championship winner Tiger Woods through 2001, 2004 Masters champion Phil Mickelson, and 2004 U.S. Open champion Retief Goosen, place their feet wider than shoulder-width apart, as did the legendary Ben Hogan before them. As friend, mentor, and former U.S. Open champion Ken Venturi taught me, the wide stance promotes a shallower swing and an elongated *flat spot* through the hitting area. The wide stance promotes resistance in the lower body and less hip turn. The more agile and flexible golfers who can still make a full shoulder turn while bracing the lower body can thus build up more torque and much more speed.

Forming a visual picture of this posture position will help you stand correctly to the ball at address.

To complete your setup, bend from the hips with your knees flexed, legs relaxed, and your shoulder and hip lines parallel to the target line. Distribute your weight evenly from the ball of each foot back to the heel of each foot. You can check this position easily in front of a full-length mirror, or at home or at many driving ranges. Incidentally, when checking your posture, pay close attention to the angle of your shoulders. You want them to be tilted at least ten degrees away from the target, but not more than thirty degrees. The front shoulder should be high and the back shoulder low to preset an upward hit.

When practicing, get in the habit of following this basic pre-swing *routine*.

CLUB POSITION/BALL POSITION

Once you adjust yourself into a comfortable address position, the clubface should be perpendicular to the target. The butt of the club, and thus your hands, should point between your navel and the crease of your slacks. Deviating from this configuration is not recommended. As long as you keep the hands and the club handle between your body center and the crease of your slacks, you're within the acceptable parameters that I teach to students who visit my schools.

Speaking of parameters, when setting up to hit a standard drive, be sure that the ball is positioned no farther behind your left heel than two inches and no farther ahead than an inch. From my experience, beginner amateurs normally hit powerfully accurate drives more consistently if they position the ball opposite the left heel.

This ball position for the drive is critically important because it will allow you to make contact at the bottom of your arc or even just a fraction after the clubhead has reached its lowest point. Believe me, even power-drivers do not swing down—they know you can't hit long drives this way. There just isn't enough loft built into the driver to launch the ball high at the optimum angle into the air if you hit with a descending blow rather than with a sweeping action. So play the ball almost directly off the left heel and your natural swing arc will allow you to sweep the ball cleanly off the tee.

I recommend that beginner players tee the ball high for the driver, at least one full inch, like Champions Tour player Bruce Lietzke does, so that more of the ball is resting atop the crown of the clubhead at address. With the new super-large driver heads,

When teaching a beginner how to hit a driver, I make a point of stressing the importance of teeing the ball up fairly high, since this position promotes confidence and a tension-free swing.

you should probably use two-and-a-half-inch tees. This tee height promotes confidence and a tension-free swinging action. Everything in your setup should encourage a sweeping action with the driver, and teeing the ball high will help you form the right mental picture. Furthermore, with the ball teed up above the crown of your driver, you virtually eliminate the possibility of catching the clubhead on the ground prior to impact and jarring the clubface from its intended line.

When playing in bad weather, unless the wind is exceptionally strong, I think you will maintain a smooth flow to your swing and hit consistent shots if you play the ball up in your stance. Moving the ball back to hit a low, boring shot is a technique more geared to the very advanced player. Furthermore, with modern equipment, even most pros keep their ball position consistent with the driver. A solid drive will work well in any conditions.

IMAGERY CONCEPTS: NON-VISUALIZATION

I played numerous tournament rounds with the famous Canadian professional Moe Norman, who is regarded as one of the best ball strikers ever. These rounds were played during the 1970s when he was still playing very well.

There were more unusual aspects of Moe Norman and his golf game. One thing I have not seen written about his great golf was his pre-shot routine. Moe did not have one. He simply went up and hit the ball; to me it looked like he used zero visualization. If I was hitting first on a tee shot, I had to pick up my tee quickly or Moe would have his ball in the air. He would walk up to his ball quickly and BAM it was gone.

I chalked this up to just another highly unusual aspect of his personality. Yet the more I thought about Moe, and the more I taught golf, I continued to flash back to Moe's lack of preparation. It was as if he had no care whatsoever, and that was the obvious key. Moe hit golf shots with no fear of results on every swing. He truly played tournament golf like he was just "beating balls" at the range. Moe hit shots with his "body mind" and not his thinking brain. I believe this is the highest form of peak performance.

A true master of anything makes his art simple. To the great ones in music, science, or sport, their perception of what they do is easy. The genius does, he does not explain. And often the genius cannot really explain his or her incredibly exceptional gift. Einstein saw a rainbow and thought of the Theory of Relativity. Monet painted a picture now worth millions in three strokes of his paintbrush. I can think of many other examples but there are three personal examples I would like to briefly share.

In my visits with legendary basketball coach John Wooden at his home, it became very apparent that he saw nothing special in what he did. I spent about ten hours of personal time with the man most authorities consider the greatest coach ever, and if there's a person more at peace with himself than John Wooden, I would like to meet that man. He was totally comfortable talking about anything as I taped conversations or took notes. Most people do not know that Coach Wooden loves golf and still follows the PGA Tour. We had great talks on golf, but I was far more interested in how he coached his basketball teams, how he handled different personalities, and how he motivated the players. To him, all of this was very simple. It was just a matter of following his system of coaching. Coach Wooden saw coaching as following a blueprint and being totally prepared. He wanted his players to be at their personal best and he worked hard to make this happen. Even when Coach Wooden had poor training facilities for his basketball teams, he visualized success, and he achieved it so greatly that nobody will likely ever surpass his achievements.

When I did my videotape on Sam Snead, I spent three days with him at his home in Hot Springs, Virginia. I also stayed in a house with Sam at the Masters and did two television shows with him on The Golf Channel.

Probably the greatest quote I ever heard about Sam was, "Watching Snead practice his golf swing was like watching a fish practice swimming." Snead came out of the hills of West Virginia with no formal training and yet had what many experts believe was the most beautiful swing ever. It is a model for most top teachers, and the swing I've heard Tiger Woods copied as a child. Snead won tour events in six decades and won the most tour events of anyone in the history of the PGA Tour (eighty-one). Snead saw golf as simple. He couldn't really explain what he did, just visualized a swing and did it without thinking. If you asked Sam how he hit a hook, he would say, "I just see the shot shape and hit it." The visualization was simple and quick. It was not intense or prepared, but rather natural and clean, more reactive.

My college roommate and great friend Bruce Lietzke is another golf genius. Bruce almost never practices, takes months off, and still makes millions of dollars playing professional golf. He played less than any tour regular, yet somehow, nearly year in and year out, he wins events and big money, basically in his spare time.

One reason for his great success is the ability to drive the ball long and straight. I've often thought about how much fun golf would be if I never had to practice and still knew I could hit the ball great. If you asked the tour professionals of his time who the best ball striker was, many would pick Bruce. If you asked them who they would trade full game shots with, many would choose Lietzke simply because no practice was required.

Bruce did not aim drivers at a tree or a particular spot on the fairway. Instead he saw the shape of the shot play out in his mind. For Bruce, that was a medium-high fade. Once he got over the ball and set up, he did something very unusual. His mind left his body. That is, he left his physical body and floated about twenty-five feet away, then he watched himself hit the shot. Nobody ever trained Bruce to do this. He cannot explain how it first happened. He never questioned this experience, but rather embraced it.

I've read about weight lifters working on this sort of out-of-body technique. I believe it is more familiar to Eastern cultures. Putting yourself as an observer who watches the mindless execution of the physical body is an unbelievably powerful way to take pressure off and remove your mind from the swing action. I believe more golfers should work to achieve this Zen type of disassociation, especially in pressure-packed situations.

The lesson I take from geniuses is to let your best performance come forth. Don't force it. Let go. Trust what you have worked on in practice. Do not question yourself on the course. Allow great things to happen.

IMAGERY CONCEPTS: STANDARD VISUALIZATION

Once you are over the ball, think in terms of *target*, whether you actually see an intermediate target yards ahead of the ball and in line with your actual target, or just imagine one. Focus on that target and then on making a free-flowing golf swing. From the moment you take this look until the instant you draw the club back, you should visualize the long, penetrating flight of the ball to that distant target. All you should see is the imaginary ball flight or that target area. When viewing the target, try to avoid letting your eyes wander to the trees, water, deep rough, or any other trouble. If this happens, and it will sometimes, simply clear your mind and then refocus on the target zone. Focus on your landing spot and maybe let one or two simple swing thoughts enter your mind, as do the greatest golfers in the world.

Your visualization process should basically be the same for wedge shots and putts: Positive and Vivid.

To help you let loose mentally, here are some of the cues used by various pros, some of which I have incorporated into my teaching.

To promote a strong turning action, load the right hip without sliding, and prevent a reverse-pivot, Greg Norman thinks "RHP," which is his signal to turn his right hip pocket back. To keep the clubface square to the target, Ken Venturi thinks, "The back of my left hand is a second clubface." At impact, his goal is to have the clubface and the back of his left hand line up. Tiger Woods was trained by John Anselmo, his longtime junior instructor, to visualize a flat left wrist position at the top of his swing, in order to take his mind off the takeaway and have him swing back smoothly and arrive in a good backswing position.

The secret of the pre-swing routine is to use your mind to line up correctly and ready yourself to make a good golf swing that delivers the club squarely and solidly to the ball. The added benefit of the pre-swing routine is that it prepares you to let go—mentally and physically. I also like to remind students that the opposite of routine is random. Random and consistent just do not go together. Just prior to swinging back, you should be taking looks at the target and waggling the club until you feel comfortable and confident enough to trigger the action. I generally teach two looks to the target and then go, a routine I learned from Johnny Revolta, who is a true golf legend. You can even get more active with the waggle and employ a miniature backswing rehearsal, as PGA Tour pros Mike Weir and Chris DeMarco do when preparing to drive the golf ball. Both of these top players make a takeaway rehearsal, actually employing a slow half backswing or a super-long waggle to help groove a pure movement away from the ball. Remember, the purpose of the routine is preparation, repetition, and relaxation. Practice these preparatory moves and your routine will become so repetitive that you will actually start completing it in precisely the same amount of time. Have a friend clock you when you are on top of your game and you'll see that it's true.

Chapter 4

THE BASIC DRIVER BACKSWING

I've determined that the absolute best way to train my students to swing the club back correctly into a powerful and correct coil, from the takeaway to the at-the-top position, is to teach them in simple steps. This position approach gives the student specific goals to achieve and time to learn and groove each step independently in practice before blending the steps together into one flowing, uninterrupted motion. It's always extremely rewarding to see phenomenal improvement in a very short time.

The backswing action I've created for my students involves four steps, although I never teach too many positions in one lesson. The first step entails moving the clubhead about three feet away from the ball. It is a step that some newcomers to golf initially think is not very important. However, they soon realize that this step sets the scene for the remainder of the swing. What it comes down to is this: Little mistakes early on in the backswing lead to big mistakes in the downswing, which create errant shots. Conversely, if you start the club back on track smoothly, you are more likely to continue to coordinate the movement of the body with the movement of the club throughout the swing and return the club to a square impact position. For this reason, let me give you some simple guidelines for successfully carrying out this vital first step, which Ben Hogan called "the first crossroad of the golf swing."

When starting Step One of the backswing, I recommend you use some slight toward-the-target motion ("forward press") to ignite your takeaway. For example, lift and replant the right heel, push your hands slightly toward the target, or shift the left hip slightly. From this micro-move forward, swing the club smoothly back, using mostly the hands, arms, and shoulders to control the action. We now move to the halfway back position. I call this the "hand back move."

Step *one* of my
8-Step Swing.

When the club is parallel to the ground and the butt-end of the grip points approximately at the target, you have completed what I consider the Step Two position of the golf swing. This is the very best backswing checkpoint position, so stop and take inventory. Monitor the action, and form a mental picture of this halfway back motion. At the Step Two position, when you're halfway through the back-

Step *two* of my
8-Step Swing.

swing, nothing should be badly trailing or leading. The club, arms, and shoulders have remained connected as a single unit and your weight has moved into the back leg. This is your *backswing package*. At Step Two, everything has worked together and you are balanced and relaxed. Also, your hands and arms should feel low, or down. It's a great feeling to simplify this section of the golf swing.

Step Three is simply the three-quarter position. When swinging into this position, again physically feel the motion, particularly in your feet and legs. Your full weight shift (of 75–90 percent) is into the middle of your right foot. Practice the balance of your backswing coil, stopping at the three-quarter point. At Step Three, your weight is fully loaded on top of a solid and flexed right knee. Your shoulders, hands, and arms have moved away smoothly. It's as if you have simply drawn the clubhead away from the target. At this three-quarter position, I want you to check a few other key points in the mirror. For example, make sure that your left wrist is nearly flat (level, with no indentation or bowing between the wrist and forearm). Make sure your left arm is nearly straight and has remained relaxed. Make sure the clubshaft is on plane, at about a forty-five-degree angle. Also, remember that the head moves laterally with the coil. In fact, your head can move a few inches away from the target, or "off the ball," while your chin also rotates. Make sure, though, that your head has remained level and has not dipped or lifted up.

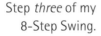

Step *three* of my
8-Step Swing.

Step *four* of my 8-Step Swing. (Note that the club is not exactly in the parallel position, but well within what I call my *Corridors of Success*, proving that I allow the golfer some leeway in what is considered a pure fundamental.)

Step Four (See page two of color insert, in the Driving Lessons segment for the Beginner Player) is marked by the completion of the back-around movement of the body and the club, just before the return move toward the target. What's most important here is the degree of shoulder turn versus hip turn.

A number of years ago, I wrote a book called *The X-Factor Swing*. (I also did a videotape and ran a ten-part series on The Golf Channel of the same name), in which I examined body angles, body moves, power keys, and how the differential or "gap" between your shoulder turn and your hip (the "X-factor") turn affects your power potential. Working with golf professional Mike McTeigue and a company called SportSense, we found that a large gap between those two turns greatly influences how far you can hit the golf ball. If you let your hips turn together in tandem with your shoulders, you're creating no resistance. That means you get less torque at the top, which translates into less speed going forward and less distance. In a power backswing, the shoulders generally turn about twice as much as the hips, so you should feel resistance in your lower body as you make your full driver backswing. To increase your X-Factor, maintain the flex in your right knee and keep freedom in your shoulder turn.

At Step Four, the upper body has completed its windup, and the uncoiling of the lower body will now lead the forward swing move. At this juncture in a full swing, a top player will rotate his shoulders nearly one hundred degrees and his hips only fifty degrees. I know backswing lengths move in a range or within "Corridors of Success," so the club can be somewhat short of parallel or past it when you reach the end of the backswing. Where the club ends up depends on one's individual talent, age, flexibility, strength, and other variables. As a matter of note, however, many great drivers swing the club past parallel. This is contrary to what many teachers recommend.

Speaking of parameters, at this stage of the swing I want to address my thoughts on a very controversial subject: the position of the right elbow.

Some golf instructors say that as the club approaches the top of the backswing, your arms should remain relatively tight to your body. They suggest that your hands and arms should remain in a rather low position, with your firm left arm remaining at the angle at which your shoulders have turned away from the ball. When your left arm is in this position, they note, your right arm will be very much tucked into your right side, with the right elbow pointing more or less down. A checkpoint that these theorists like to use is this: if you are in what they term a "connected" position, you should be able to place a handkerchief underneath your right armpit and make a complete backswing without the handkerchief dropping. This advice is often overdone, and the student winds up with a narrow backswing and no power.

As you can see from this down-target view of Step *four*, I prefer the golfer to have some space between his right elbow and body when reaching the top of the backswing.

On the other end, the flying or winging right elbow is the source of a lot of controversy in the golf swing. It's been stated many times that a winging elbow means that the swing is not on plane, that it's too upright. The fact is many great players have flying right elbows, most notably Jim Furyk, Fred Couples, and Jack Nicklaus. I just don't buy the theory that there is one perfect plane on which everybody ought to swing the club back on, and I base my opinion on studying hundreds of great drivers. There is no one perfect backswing position, and you can easily prove this to yourself by even casually observing today's PGA Tour players, or looking back and recalling the swings of two golf giants, Ben Hogan and Jack Nicklaus. Hogan's swing was very low, while Nicklaus's is very upright. In summary, no two swings were alike then, and no two swings are exactly alike now—in both the top amateur and professional arenas.

Nicklaus's right elbow winged out dramatically, and this so-called fault caused him to be taken to task by golf critics. However, Jack managed to win eight major championships by the time he was twenty-six, so that quieted a lot of people. And it proved that his upright swing worked. He won twenty major championships (if you count his two U.S. Amateur victories) and is regarded by most golf experts as the greatest golfer ever. I know Jack is number one on my list.

One last important point: In 1993, *The Eight-Step Swing* was published with a phrase that really caught on, influencing other teachers, students, and tour players: "When the shoulders stop turning, the arms stop swinging." Really think about this, and realize that what I'm emphasizing is that in a good backswing, the arms and shoulders reach the top at the same time.

Finally, allow me to review some critical top-of-the-backswing checkpoints:

- Make a full shoulder turn.
- The left shoulder turns under the chin.
- The right shoulder turns behind the right ear.
- Sense your hands swinging over the right shoulder.
- At the top of the backswing, the clubshaft will point somewhere near the target. This is always a key image.
- The clubface alignment at the top varies in great drivers from open (toe down) to closed (clubface pointing skyward). For all average golfers, I

much prefer a squared to slightly closed clubface at the top. It is much more powerful. Most of golf's greatest all-time drivers had the clubface square or closed at the top.

- Maintain constant grip pressure from address to the top. If you start at pressure "four," then be at pressure "four" when you reach the completion of your backswing. Many amateurs loosen their grip near the top.
- There is no actual stop at the top. As you reach the top of the backswing with the shoulder turn and swing of the club, your lower body has already started forward. You do the same thing when throwing a rock or in hitting a ball in baseball or tennis.
- Think "smooth" on your backswing. No quick, fast moves.
- Stay relaxed mentally.

Chapter 5

THE BASIC DRIVER DOWNSWING

When hitting drives, or any full shot with a long club, the downswing is by far the most important part of the swing. The best downswing is almost totally a reflexive, reactive movement. It is essentially a result of what you established through a sound, relaxed setup position and a smooth, complete coiling action of the body during the backswing. However, even the most perfect backswing can be ruined by an improper start of the forward swing.

Many amateur golfers struggle with the downswing because they try so hard to create speed. I want you to work hard to avoid this very common mistake. The initial move forward begins with the lower body, not the shoulders. It is a timing move. You are not throwing the hands, arms, and shoulders hard from the top of the backswing, even though this seems natural and correct. The initial move down to the ball should feel smooth and perhaps even slow. A good start-down movement has a slight drift forward of everything with the lower body leading.

You release the club freely at the bottom of the swing to obtain maximum clubhead speed and consistent clubhead delivery. Therefore, when practicing and learning the vital steps of the downswing, I suggest you think of three simple buzzwords—*Shift, Rotate, Throw*—to start the forward move into the impact zone. These three words are vitally important because they define an athletic action. Some of you may find that you'll need to emphasize one of these swing keys more than the other two to deliver the club squarely and powerfully into the ball at impact. *Shift* means that you start the forward swing by transferring weight. This might be a lateral bump of the left hip forward or a shifting of the knees toward the target. Almost at the same time, you begin turning your hips.

Step *five* of my 8-Step Swing. Here, I'm holding my position as a checkpoint.

Then and only then comes the unleashing of the hands and arms. Please understand, though, that this downswing action occurs in a flash.

When you go through the moves of a powerful downswing as I define them, picture my descriptions vividly in your mind a few times and then take hundreds of practice swings without a ball. Over time, you'll swing with virtually no thought at all.

A key practice move is what I call a "check-swing" position. You make a full turn, complete the backswing, and then begin to move down toward the ball only to stop halfway down and check the position of the club. This is a move that golf's number-one player, Vijay Singh, uses in his daily practice sessions.

Since the most important part of the downswing is the transition move (when you change direction, from going back to starting down), I have my students practice the check-swing drill over and over until the swing operates essentially on automatic pilot. This pump type of drill, in which you practice the correct moves before impact, is extremely helpful.

If there's one secret to employing a good swing and hitting good shots, it truly occurs at this stage of the golf swing. The downswing starts with the hips/lower body "core" moving toward the target. The shoulder motion, good or bad, is a responsive motion that ties in with the hips or lower body. The lateral hip-slide or bump is not always natural to the golfer. As mentioned before, there is a tendency for many golfers to hit from the top and/or overuse the shoulders. I want you to do just the opposite. Practice using the feet, knees, and hips, so that the shoulders stay back and remain relaxed and are poised to follow.

At Step Five, the halfway down position (see page two of the color insert, in the Driving Lessons segment for the Beginner Player), make sure that when you're doing your checking, either with the help of a friend or when watching yourself on video, that the body shifts forward. Here, the weight is now centered. Weight has transferred and is evenly displaced or somewhat on the forward leg. The clubshaft is parallel to the target line. You're in position to smash the golf ball.

Step Six or Impact (see page two of color insert, in the Driving Lessons segment for the Beginner Player), Step Seven (Early Follow-Through), and Step Eight (Finish and Rebound) happen so quickly that they are impossible to consciously control. Therefore, what I would like you to do is what I and other professional and amateur golfers have done at my teaching centers since the early 1980s at New York's Sunningdale Golf Club. We watched film of great golfers at impact and right through into the finish. Here, I would like you to study these sequence photographs, first to understand them intellectually by visualizing each, and second by physically rehearsing and memorizing each move so that

Steps *six* and *seven* of my 8-Step Swing.

you will be able to blend them into a nice, flowing athletic motion. These slow-motion practice moves help you attain your ultimate goal of returning the clubface squarely and solidly into the ball at impact and hitting a powerfully accurate drive.

Step *eight* of my 8-Step Swing: Finish and Rebound

Chapter 6

DOWNSWING DRILLS FOR CLOSING THE GAP

BASEBALL DRILL

Set up normally to a teed-up ball, using a middle-iron.

Slide your left foot back toward the right, so that they practically touch each other and the clubhead is about ten inches behind the ball.

Start the backswing. When the club reaches about waist level, step toward the target with your left foot, returning it to its original position, like a batter stepping into a pitch.

The clubhead will still be moving back after the lower body moves forward, which automatically increases wrist work, prevents the right shoulder from leading the downswing, and helps you feel that fluid sensation that all great swingers experience.

RIGHT SHOULDER DOWN DRILL

Move the right shoulder downward at the start of the forward swing. This trigger encourages the hips to shift laterally toward the target. It also lowers the right elbow beneath the left arm and drops the club into the ideal position. Now you can hit from the inside, like all top tour players.

See how dropping the right shoulder downward triggers a super hip-shift toward the target—one of Ben Hogan's power secrets. Hogan knew that this shift guarantees an inside delivery.

FAN THE FOOT DRILL

Assume your normal address position. Next, widen your stance by placing your right foot well outside your right shoulder. Fan the right foot outward, so it points away from you at a forty-five-degree angle.

Hit practice shots from this position to help you eliminate any upper-body slide. It maintains a wide gap between your knees by dramatically slowing right leg action. Most of all, it helps you close the gap we talked about earlier and ultimately swing fluidly into impact and then through into the finish.

Set up like this, with your right foot fanned out dramatically, then swing. Practicing this drill will yield many benefits, including helping you learn to slow right leg action and swing fluidly through impact.

Chapter 7

ALLEVIATING TENSION

As my teachers and I tell students, *Body tension kills the golf swing and prevents you from reaching your full potential as a player.* When your muscles are tight, you have little chance of swinging the golf club rhythmically, and this means weak, off-line shots.

Golfers like you have the potential to hit much better drives and shoot lower scores by reducing the tension level in your neck, shoulders, elbows, and hands. But if you repeatedly make the same on-course mistakes, it is natural for you to tense up as a result. I want to review the classic mistakes and provide you with corrective measures, since these will help you relax.

Common Mistake: You rush the pre-swing routine and get so nervous on the teeing ground that your practice swing is a nervous swat, rather than a technically sound physical preview of the actual swing to come.

Corrective Measure: *Employ a smooth practice swing, because it's critical that you feel the sensation of the clubhead swishing. If you're unable to get the action just right on the first go, take a deep breath and make a couple of more swings until you find the one that you want to match when the time comes to hit the ball. That way, you'll feel more confident and physically relaxed.*

Common Mistake: You become so worried about where not to hit the drive that you let a negative thought enter your mind and, as a result, end up hitting the ball into trouble.

Corrective Measure: *Put a positive thought in your mind. It never hurts to visualize a great shot. Find out what works best for you. It might be to visualize the trajectory and flight of your shot. It might be to pick a small target or a wider target zone.*

It might just be a matter of picking a simple phrase like "Relax and let go" to promote a positive attitude. Experiment to determine what works best for you.

Common Mistake: You tend to worry so much about hitting a good drive—and suffering from embarrassment if you hit a bad shot—that you freeze over the ball. In short, your muscles tighten so that you make a stiff, robotic swing and hit the ball a short distance—due to a lack of arm-speed—and off-line, too, due to your failure to return the clubface squarely to the ball at impact.

    Corrective Measure: *Breathe in and out slowly a few times and imagine that your arms are made out of spaghetti or rope. When the arms are relaxed, the hands are relaxed. Consequently, you gain a good feel for the clubhead and generate a high degree of arm-speed during the swing. The result? Strong, on-line tee shots.*

Common Mistake: You start to analyze your swing in the middle of a round. The result: mental stress and body stiffness. Trying to think out a picture-perfect swing leads to paralysis by analysis. In short, you make a quick, rigid swinging motion, instead of employing a tension-free swing.

    Corrective Measure: *Picture a good swing. Often, the picture of your favorite pro golfer swinging can help immensely. Experienced players see the image of their model swing, with all its vital elements, then let go and trust it. So should you.*

Common Mistake: You start worrying about your score and thinking ahead so much that you become tense. Because you don't stay in the present, you lose your concentration and fail to hit good drives.

    Corrective Measure: *Focus on the shot at hand, not the score. If you concentrate on the process and not the outcome, you'll see that the outcome—good drives and good scores—will come. The old adage about taking "one shot at a time" is time-tested and true.*

Common Mistake: You get angry after a bad tee shot off the first tee—so angry, in fact, that you let the bad drive affect your entire day of golf. In anger, you swing so hard on every tee shot that you lose your balance and hit off-line drives for the entire round.

    Corrective Measure: *Once you hit a bad drive off the first tee, there is nothing* *you can do about it. Try to relax as you walk up the fairway, and think about other good drives you have hit in the past, or simply the beautiful scenery. This strategy will keep you relaxed and in the game mentally so you'll be ready to hit a good shot on the next tee.*

Alternatively, drop back into a 3-metal club or even a 5-metal on the next tee. These clubs are easier to control and hit solid. Once you hit a few good tee shots, go back to the driver.

Chapter 8

PRACTICE CHECKPOINTS

In order to improve at golf, you must practice intelligently, and when working on your driving game, that means checking the basic elements of the setup described in Chapter 3 and making sure that the basic swing positions reviewed in Chapters 4 and 5 are on track. You can do this by visiting your local golf professional, making an annual visit to one of my golf schools, standing and swinging in front of a mirror, or having your swing videotaped and then reviewing it. Let's now review the fine points, starting with the address position, or setup.

BASIC SETUP CHECKPOINTS

Take a driver and align your body and the club to a distant target. Next, have a friend lay a club across your toe-line and a second club behind the ball, along the target line.

If the club across your feet is parallel to the target line club, and the clubface is perpendicular to the target that you designated, you are perfectly square.

On the other hand, if your feet and body are aimed left of the target, your alignment is too open. This setup will usually promote an out-to-in swing path and a left-to-right rather than straight shot. If your bodyline is well to the right of target, you are aligned in an exaggerated closed position instead of the ideal square position.

Should your friend observe that the clubface is aiming right of the target, your hands are probably positioned too far ahead of the ball.

Once you know your mistakes, step away and start all over again, this time lining up to a short intermediate target some five yards in front of the ball. This visual adjustment will often promote square bodylines.

If you aim at an interim target some five yards ahead of the ball, it will allow you to set up like this, with square bodylines. Just do it!

BASIC SWING CHECKPOINTS

Take your driver and set up correctly to the ball, as explained in Chapter 3. Next, review the eight swing positions put forth and explained in Chapters 4 and 5 and cited here again in a more condensed form. Furthermore, in contrast to what was shown earlier, swing positions will be presented from the down-target angle.

Step One—*The First Move in the Backswing:* When the clubhead is approximately three feet from the ball, check to see if the clubshaft is still between your arms. This is a basic, non-angular, one-piece move.

The first move in the backswing: Step One.

Step Two—*Halfway Back:* Ideally, the toe of the club should be pointing up-ward.

The halfway back position: Step Two.

Step Three—*Three-Quarter Backswing Position:* The club and your left arm should form an "L."

The three-quarter backswing position: Step Three.

Step Four—*Backswing Completed:* Your shoulders are coiled and your body is balanced and loaded. The lower body provides the necessary resistance needed to create torque in the body and powerful clubface-to-ball contact.

The completion of the backswing: Step Four.

Step Five—*The Crucial Move Down To The Ball:* The arms fall and the clubshaft is on-plane.

The crucial move down to the ball: Step Five.

Step Six—*Impact:* The left wrist is flat or slightly arched.

The impact position: Step Six.

Step Seven—*Early Follow-Through:* The clubhead arcs back inside the target line.

The early follow-through position: Step Seven.

Step Eight—*Finish and Rebound:* Your hips and shoulders are fully rotated. The clubshaft swings behind your head momentarily before returning or rebounding to a relaxed, balanced position in front of your body.

The finish and rebound: Step Eight.

DRIVING INSTRUCTIONS FOR MID-LEVEL GOLFERS

Chapter 1

A DIFFERENT TYPE OF CLUB SELECTION

Mid-level players tend to want to make the jump too quickly to the Advanced category, particularly when choosing a driver. The intermediate player often purchases an extra-long, low-lofted, stiff-shafted driver, and this choice of club turns out to be a big mistake. A forty-five-inch or longer driver is often too cumbersome for most mid-level golfers to swing along the correct path on the correct plane. The shaft is too firm, so the player's swing lacks ample clubhead speed and the release action of the swing is definitely hindered. The player comes into the ball well from the inside, and because he or she can't release the shaft freely the face returns to an open position at impact. Add to this an eight-degree loft on the clubface, and your drives will be flying into water, trees, or deep rough to the right of the fairway. In the end, this means several double-bogeys per round.

To improve your play and hit long drives down the fairway, follow these instructions: Purchase a forty-four-inch driver with 10.5 degrees of loft, a medium-flex shaft, and a grip that's on the thin side to encourage a free release of the club in the impact zone.

The golfer who *knows* he or she has been fitted with the proper clubshaft is confident he can release the club freely into the ball from the downswing position shown here.

Chapter 2

SWING FICTION

Throughout my teaching career I've noticed that one of the obstacles preventing mid-level players from evolving into advanced players is that they believe practically everything they hear or read about the swing. In contrast, the low-handicap advanced player, like the pro, has the experience to ignore most tips.

To save you time in separating fact from fiction, and to expedite the learning process, I want you to study this list of swing fallacies. Make a note of where you went wrong and make the logical correction based on my comments, and you will be a step closer to attaining Advanced status.

Swing Fiction: Top-Ten List

1. Let your arms hang straight down from your shoulders when you set up to the ball. **WRONG!** *The arms should be angled somewhat outward, especially with your driver. I like to see the right forearm nearly parallel to the shaft angle.*

2. Barely grasp the club with your right hand, as if you were gently holding a bird. **WRONG!** *On my 1–10 grip pressure scale, you should be around 4 or 5.*

3. Keep your head up at address. **WRONG!** *The head should be angled slightly downward, so that your eyes can focus on the ball and your neck muscles are relaxed. Keep your chin up—that's better advice.*

4. Keep your head still throughout the swing motion. **WRONG!** *The head will drift or slide away from the target with the coil of the body. The head goes where the body takes it. The eyes and head release forward and up after impact.*

5.   You must keep your left arm straight on the backswing. **WRONG!** *Some of the greatest tee-shot players in the world, such as Fred Funk, let the left arm bend slightly. The bottom line: avoid tension and stiffness in the left arm.*

6.   When your wrists are hinged at the three-quarter position in the back-swing, the butt of the club should point at the ball. **WRONG!** *The butt of the club should be aimed at a point well behind the ball.*

7.   Pull the club down and through the ball with your hands and arms. **WRONG!** *Pulling or dragging the club down can reduce speed, keep the club-face open, and cause slice shots. There are equal degrees of push and pull in a good golf swing.*

8.   Swing the club down the target line. **WRONG!** *The club swings into a square impact position, then starts moving inside or to the left of the target.*

Here are four examples of fictitious fundamentals to avoid if you want to improve at golf and reach the next level of play:

1. Keep your head up at address.
2. Keep your left arm straight on the backswing.
3. Pull the club down and through the ball with your hands and arms.
4. Finish high.

9.   Finish high. **WRONG!** *The best drivers on the PGA Tour, such as two-time U.S. Open champion Retief Goosen, finish low and around. Furthermore, at the end of the swing the clubshaft also often rests on their neck, proving that their arms are relaxed and tension-free throughout the motion.*

Chapter 3

CORRECT BODY ANGLES, POSITIONS, AND PIVOT ACTIONS

The golf swing can be a very complex and dynamic action if broken down by an expert, or it can be simplified and work essentially automatically. You especially see this in young junior golfers who quickly pick up the game and swing with reckless abandon. It's beautiful to watch. That's what we want for you as a player. If your angles and positions are correct at address, most other details will fall into place automatically.

The clearer you appreciate the setup picture mentally and the better you feel the angles and positions physically, the better you'll be able to make great progress and reach a higher level. Right now, however, let's review the paramount angles and body positions of the address position, and then the pivot actions relative to the backswing and downswing.

DRIVING ADDRESS ANGLES AND POSITIONS

The most important body positions at address involve the angle of your feet, spine, and head.

When setting up, you more flexible golfers can box your right foot in so that it is perpendicular to the target line. This position will allow you to make a full and fluid turn of the hips without over-turning and draining power from your swing. Turn your left foot outward ten to thirty degrees, which will promote a free counterclockwise clearing action of the left hip on the downswing and open up a passageway for the arms and hands to swing the club freely through the ball.

As far as posture is concerned, you should create about a twenty- to thirty-degree angle between the legs and spine when bending forward from the hips.

This starting position helps you stand the proper distance from the golf ball, coil more fluidly and freely, and greatly increase your chance of hitting a good drive.

Position the head by keeping the neck relaxed and your chin up off your chest. You can check this by making a fist with your left hand and placing it under your chin. There should be ample space between your chin and chest. If you can't get your fist under your chin, tilt your head up slightly. Your eyes should be parallel to the target line, meaning that the head is held straight without angles. Remember, I'm only talking about the setup; during the swing, particularly going back, your head will likely move several inches, with your chin rotating as well.

When setting up, you should create about a 20- 30-degree angle between the legs and spine.

Now that you have a clear understanding of the body positions at address, I want to review the pivot actions of the backswing and downswing. Understand, however, that I'm only covering the essentials here.

As you read my instructions, I want to make it perfectly clear that these positions are simply good guidelines. By now, you know I believe in giving a player leeway. Stay within my corridors, because minor variations are acceptable.

BACKSWING PIVOT

Footwork: As the backswing begins, there is first a feeling of a slight weight shift off the inside of the left instep, with a constant increase of weight shift to the in-

As I move from the address position *(left)* to the backswing position *(right)*, note the movements of the feet, knees, hips, shoulders, and head. Note, too, how the shoulders turn more than the hips, creating powerful X-Factor torque.

side of the right foot (toward the right heel) and right leg. I like to see the weight shift occur early in the backswing. Think of a move to the side, not an immediate turn.

It's okay, on long shots, for the left heel to lift a few inches off the ground during a full driver backswing, provided it is pulled off the ground. More flexible players, however, should leave the left foot planted.

Knee Action: Your knee action and knee turn pretty much dictate the degree of hip rotation during the backswing. Proper knee motion involves both knees. On the backswing, the left knee breaks inward and outward simultaneously. It simply stays in sync with the total release of the entire left side in your takeaway. Remember, the left knee does not pop straight out, nor does it slide back toward the right knee.

The right knee action is critical to the bracing of the entire right leg and hip. The right knee does not totally freeze in place; in fact it's a plus if you can maintain the same flex throughout the backswing. I do not like to see the right knee lock up—I like to see the flex in the right knee maintained.

Hip Action: The lower body should resist the turning of the upper body during the backswing (to create torque). Think of it as a spring being wound in your hips and torso. Less hip movement on the backswing (see page four of color insert in the Driving Lessons segment for the Mid-Level Player), around forty to sixty-five degrees, usually translates into a more powerful movement on the forward swing.

Shoulder Movement: The shoulders turn on an axis perpendicular to your spine. This means the left shoulder goes down in the backswing while the right shoulder goes up. It's often useful to visualize the shoulders turning twice as much as the hips. When you correctly turn your shoulders, you'll feel the right shoulder moving up and behind your head while the left shoulder moves slightly downward and behind the ball. All top players turn their shoulders on an axis. The left shoulder does not move level.

Head Movement: The head turns and/or moves to the right slightly. It has to or the pivot will be so tense that you won't be able to employ a free, athletic backswing action. In a full swing, a top player rotates the chin to the right twenty to twenty-five degrees away from the target.

DOWNSWING PIVOT

Footwork: The weight shifts from the right post to the left post, off the inside of the right foot. This is crucial to employing the two-pivot swing and a flat spot in the impact zone. Many great players, particularly the great Sam Snead, pushed off the right foot to trigger the downswing pivot action and put a little more power into their shots when reaching impact (see page four of color insert, in the Driving Lessons for the Mid-Level Player).

Knee Action: The typical mid-level player who attends our schools has too much knee action in the backswing and too little in the downswing. In contrast,

Visualize and rehearse these downswing positions, so that when you have a club in your hand you swing fluidly through them naturally, without swing thoughts running through your brain.

the modern-day professional resists with the lower body, then really uses the ground and the knees to pump forward into the finish.

Hip Action: As the right knee moves outward in front of the ball, weight shifts. This is due to the lateral motion in the forward swing. Then, as the hips begin to rise through impact, they also rotate diagonally left. As the body fully releases and your weight is fully forward, the hips actually turn left of the target. These hip movements happen in an instant, so I prefer that you simply think of a diagonal rotation of the hips and try to finish tall.

Shoulder Movement: The stored energy in the upper torso (created by the X-Factor gap between the hip and shoulder turns), plus the initiation of the lower body, causes the shoulders to follow and then unwind with tremendous force. Remember, keep your left shoulder closed as you allow the hip muscles and your body-core to lead the forward swing.

Head Movement: Around twenty years ago, multiple major-championship winner and avid student of the swing Johnny Miller emphasized to me the importance of the head pivoting. Miller believes, like I do, that the head has its own miniature swing, moving away from the target on the backswing nearly re-centering at impact, then moving toward the target on the downswing. Without any doubt, the head moves in a great swing. Do not lock your head. Do not keep your head down. Do not think of your head as a central immovable post. And realize that in the finish of the swing, you will be standing tall with your head considerably higher than it was at address (see page four of color insert, in the Driving Lessons segment for the Mid-Level Player). That's first-grade golf talk!

Chapter 4

HOW TO HIT THE DRAW-DRIVE

While the fade is sometimes the advanced player's popular choice of tee shot, the draw is the shot I prefer to teach most students, particularly mid-level golfers, to incorporate into their repertoire. Why? Since we stand to the side of the ball, the club should naturally swing inside, down the target line and then

When playing the draw-drive, tee up near the left side marker. Furthermore, the more you want the ball to curve, the farther right you should aim your body. Here, I'm setting up for a big draw.

back to the inside. Because you come into impact like a soccer-style kicker in football, the natural ball flight should be a draw.

The draw shot flies on a low trajectory, so it's ideal in the wind. This shot lands with less spin, too, so it rolls farther than a fade, which is a great advantage for increasing distance. The added distance you pick up will allow you to attack the flag with a lofted short iron on many more par-four holes. These clubs are easier to hit than a medium or long iron, so you'll stand a much better chance of hitting the ball close to the hole and scoring birdie. On par-five holes, longer drives allow you the opportunity to reach the green in two and have a run at an eagle.

When setting up to play the draw-drive, stand on the left side of the tee. Align your feet, knees, hips, and shoulders toward the right side of the fairway—where you want the ball to start its flight. To guarantee a draw, aim the clubface at the center of the fairway, where you want the ball to end up most of the time. What you are doing is actually closing the clubface. The more right-to-left spin you want to put on the ball, the farther right you should aim your body and the more you should close the clubface.

By presetting for a draw and then swinging, you'll cause the ball to fly off the clubface on a flat trajectory, hard down the right side of the fairway, and then turn to the center of the fairway. Once the ball hits the short grass it will take off hard and fast, giving you more distance.

Chapter 5

HOW TO HIT THE CONTROLLED HOT HOOK

Some of you mid-level players who have good control over your body and the club, and who consider yourself to be "feel" players, might do well to try to hit the hot hook shot. This shot has the same advantages as the soft draw, except that it will turn even faster in the air and roll farther upon landing. It's ideal for cutting the corner on a dogleg left and really shortening a long hole.

The controlled hook does require superb timing, but if you practice the following method you will be able to play the shot and reap the rewards.

When setting up to play this shot, tee the ball very high, like former British Open champion Justin Leonard, so that when it sits on the peg you put into the ground it is totally above the top of the driver's face. This raised tee position promotes a flat arc of swing, which allows your hands and forearms to roll over through impact more easily. In turn, the clubface rolls over at impact, thereby allowing you to impart heavy right-to-left over-spin on the ball.

To further encourage a shallow swing plane, strengthen your grip by turning both hands a hair clockwise, until the Vs formed by each thumb and forefinger point to your right shoulder as you set the driver behind the ball. The clubhead is thus soled in such a way that its face is looking well right of the target, to allow for the hook.

To promote a very active, free, and natural turn of the right hip on the backswing (in order to make room for the club to swing on a flatter plane), set your right foot back a couple of inches from the normal square position. When aiming, close your stance and your body lines but keep the clubface aimed directly at the corner of the dogleg, where the hole starts to curve dramatically to the left.

Since you will want to extend the club back low and inside the target line to promote a powerful arc on the backswing, assume a wider stance. Some good players visualize an imaginary pyramid, formed by lines running from the outside of the heels to the outside of the shoulders, in order to build a strong base to swing from.

Before going on to the swing keys involved, I want to make a few things clear.

The first thing you need to understand and visualize is the shape of the arc required to hit this shot. Second, you must be able to control the clubface. You cannot have the face open through impact and hit the ball right-to-left.

To understand the proper arc, I want you to visualize the high bank turns at the Indianapolis 500 or on a roller derby track. Actually see the curve in your mind's eye as you stand at address readying yourself to swing. Once you have this image fixed in your mind, imagine the club turning with that curve. Furthermore, just before you swing, see your right arm making this rounded curve in the follow-through, since this will ultimately promote the correct release action and the desired shape of the shot.

To maximize the width of your backswing arc, don't be afraid to move off the ball slightly to the right, away from the target, as soon as you trigger the takeaway. This key increases the distance the clubhead travels and thereby creates a wide and powerful swing arc.

You may need to consciously rip the clubhead through impact with your forearms and hands until you build sufficient confidence. Now it's time to make that last link in the power chain work for you.

When learning how to hit the hot hook, practice covering the ball with the toe of the club, as I'm doing here. You don't need to hit balls right away. Practice in your workstation until you get a good feel for a free release action and the toe of the club leading the heel through impact.

Whipping the club into the ball with your hands, arms, and wrists is crucial to hitting the hot hook successfully, as is letting the toe of the driver win the race to the ball. My teachers and I call this "covering the ball with the toe." It's a semi-advanced idea first conceived by Ken Venturi, but when you get it, the hot hook will be a tremendous weapon to have in your shot-making arsenal.

Chapter 6

WHAT TO DO WHEN DRIVING IN WINDY CONDITIONS

HEADWIND STRATEGIES

When driving into a headwind, you must be mentally disciplined enough to do exactly the opposite of what you feel you should do: You must swing easily instead of hard. The harder you swing at the ball, the more backspin the club will impart on it. This is true with the driver as well as with the wedges. The faster you swing at the driver and the more backspin you apply, the more the headwind will work under the ball, pushing it farther upward in its flight. The higher it flies, the more it hangs before dropping steeply to the ground so that it gets little or no roll. Also, wild shots curve even more in windy conditions.

When driving into a very strong wind, you want to hit a tee shot with a relatively low, boring flight and less backspin so that the wind never works its way under the ball. The best way to obtain this dart-like trajectory is to tee the ball lower and swing the driver easier, visualizing a swing like Ernie Els's or the late Payne Stewart's.

DOWNWIND STRATEGIES

The main objective in driving downwind, provided a lake or other trouble spot is not within reach, is to take advantage of this condition. You want to launch your tee shot on a higher angle than normal, so you get more air under the ball early and a bigger boost from the wind. You need only to make a few small adjustments in your setup and swing to get added height.

Tee the ball higher than you normally do. With the wind at your back you should also play the ball two inches forward of its normal position, so that it's opposite your left instep rather than the left heel. Distribute your weight so it's a little more on your right foot. Also, lower your right shoulder and set your head slightly further back.

Once you are set up in a comfortably correct position, concentrate on making a slow takeaway action and a full backswing. These adjustments will cause you to contact the ball with your driver moving into the upswing, rather than level with the ground. This will effectively add two to three degrees of loft to the clubface at impact. The higher launch angle can easily give you twenty to thirty extra yards on your drive, and even more with a really strong wind at your back.

CROSSWIND STRATEGIES

The safest way for you to play tee shots in a crosswind is to aim your ball to the side of the target from which the wind is blowing and let the wind work it back. For example, if a wind of about twenty miles per hour is blowing from the left, aim twenty yards left of the centerline, then simply let the wind drift the ball back to the "short grass."

Alternatively, you could play a draw in a right-to-left crosswind or a fade in a left-to-right crosswind, as a means of riding the wind and picking up as much as thirty yards of added yardage. This is an excellent tactic on long holes that offer plenty of room, provided you remember to aim farther left when playing in a strong fade-wind and farther right when playing in strong draw-wind.

Chapter 7
MIND GAMES

I've seen more and more good players and pros improve their fairways-hit percentages by changing their swing, but it never ceases to amaze me how an intermediate, mid-level player can sometimes make the jump into the Advanced category without revamping their existing technique.

How do they do this? The golfer does some physical things like teeing up on the correct side of the tee box, and on level ground, plus shaking tension out of his wrists and fingers. More importantly, though, good players simply work hard on the mental game. For example, just before swinging, he or she imagines the speed of the swing gradually increasing, from takeaway to impact, sort of like a jet moving from a standstill and reaching high speed at the end of the runway.

What follows are some other mental tips that can improve your driving game.

1. Before setting up, recall a good drive you hit previously on the same hole or a similar-looking one. It cannot hurt to recall super-positive images and boast confidence.

2. Stand behind the ball and pick out a landing spot in an area of fairway grass, then see your drive flying toward that target. Some golfers do very well with precise trajectory.

3. Walk into the shot confidently, with positive, pro-like body language.

4. At address, mentally clean the slate of any previously hit bad drives. Wait until any negative images clear from your mind. If they should pop into

your head, step away and start your routine all over again or even go back to the golf bag for a total re-start.

5. You can also try the Moe Norman approach of paying little attention to targets. If you are a golfer who sees the bunkers and hazards, glancing out to the general target will work well for you. My own experience in playing with Moe Norman, a fairway hitting machine, tells me this idea can really work.

6. Visualize the ball flying off the clubface through a Hula Hoop or doorway several yards in front of you, because seeing your line of flight will encourage you to swing your club along it.

7. Let a key positive thought enter your mind before you swing.

8. Imagine what legendary player and teacher Jack Burke, Jr., told me in order to promote a tension-free, uninhibited swinging action: Make believe you are driving into the Pacific Ocean, not trying to hit a narrow fairway. In other words, make a "let go" free swing. Be more reckless. Remember, a true swing has no guide in it.

Chapter 8

FIVE DYNAMITE DRIVING DRILLS

If you have read my previous books or *Golf Digest* magazine articles, watched me give lessons on The Golf Channel, or visited one of my schools around the country, you know that a central focal point of my teaching is devoted to practice drills. In fact, I recently wrote a second book dedicated entirely to practice drills: Golf Digest*'s Ultimate Drill Book*.

I've discussed drills for every area of the game, but since we're talking about driving in this section, I'd like to teach you five dynamite drills for improving your tee-shot skills. Read these over carefully and study the photographs, so that you do the right thing in practice and become ready to do the right thing on the course.

DRILL # 1: SWING-UNDER-THE-SHAFT DRILL

Purpose: To teach you to move the club back in a low, more streamlined fashion, which is the first step in creating a wide and powerful swing arc. To teach you to enter the impact zone on a shallow arc, so that a flat spot is created and square clubface-to-ball contact is guaranteed. To teach you a *guaranteed inside approach* to the ball that will help you eliminate the slice.

Set up like this for the Swing-Under-the-Shaft drill. Next, swing the club back and through *under* the shaft, in the takeaway and the hit-zone.

Procedure: Stick a shaft through a range-ball basket or miniature golf bag. Swing the driver back under the shaft. Once you get a feel for the "under" actions, swing and hit balls. You don't need to buy any fancy training aid; I've used this drill for thirty years, and it works.

DRILL # 2: RIGHT-ARM-ONLY ON-CENTER DRILL

Purpose: To learn the true meaning of right-side power in the golf swing and hit solid, on-target drives with a full release.

Procedure: Set up with your left forefinger or left-hand fingers in the center of your chest. Grip down on the club with your right hand only. Swing back with your coil and right arm in synchronization. Let the right arm swing and fold into a right angle, so that the elbow moves together with your shoulder and the movement of your body center in the area of the sternum. The arm and the shoulder coil should arrive at the top of the backswing together.

Swing down, concentrating on swinging the right arm down close to the body and coordinating the movement with that of your body center right through into the finish. You should hear a nice swishing sound near the hitting area, and the clubhead should accelerate in the impact zone to the finish. If you hear the swish too early, you have released the right hand too soon.

The Right-Arm-Only On-Center drill: In Sequence.

DRILL # 3: RIGHT–ARM–TOSS DRILL

Purpose: To teach you to employ the correct right-arm, right-shoulder movements, so that you come into the ball from the inside instead of the outside, and hit straight shots rather than slices.

    This drill, taught to me by former Masters and PGA champion Jack Burke, Jr., will also help you learn to properly sequence lower-body action with the correct throwing motion during the swing. Jack Burke's father, one of the greatest teachers in America, often used this drill for training students. So it is an idea that has worked well for decades.

Procedure: Grip the club in your right hand only. Take your address position, then look down the fairway and pick out a specific target.

    Swing the club back to the three-quarter position.

    Start the downswing by taking a small step forward with your left foot, then actually throw the club on a line drive at the target using an underhand/sidearm

throwing motion. I've used this drill with tour players, so it's not a joke. Get to a safe area, free of any people, and work on straight line-drive throws. Don't worry about breaking a club. It won't happen. Still, many students find this drill much more difficult than expected, so start easy. A good throw will go at least thirty yards and will be directly at your target. This drill is guaranteed to produce good results.

DRILL # 4: TEE-HEIGHT DRILL

Purpose: To promote a shallow swing arc, a longer flat spot through impact, and more penetrating drives that draw.

Procedure: Take your normal setup position for a drive, then tee the ball up very high (at least one inch above the turf). Now replace your driver with a three-metal or five-metal. Next, line up the clubface level with the ball, which means the clubhead will be above the grass.

When teaching my students (even tour professionals) the Right-Arm-Toss drill, I tell them that throwing a club can be good for your golf game.

Swing back at seventy-five percent of your normal speed. Next, concentrate on sweeping the ball cleanly off the tee. With the much smaller clubhead, this drill is far more difficult than you think. The idea is to sweep the ball off the tee.

This drill will instantly reveal your swing flaws. A miss with the shallow-faced fairway metal will result in a pop-up.

When working on this drill, which I use frequently with students looking to improve their driving game, you may find that a higher tee height, like that used by Sergio Garcia, will give you the confidence to make a stronger windup off the body, swing on a shallower plane, and hit more powerful tee shots.

DRILL # 5: HEAVY DUTY WORKOUT DRILL

Purpose: To help you stretch and strengthen vital golf muscles and accelerate the driver in the impact zone for more distance.

Procedure: The majority of golf shops and retail outlets sell weighted clubs that are usually the same length as a standard men's driver. The clubhead, the shaft, or both are heavily weighted with sand or lead so that the club weighs about five times what a normal driver would—four to five pounds instead of twelve or thirteen ounces.

Swing the training club every day in your backyard or indoor workout area. The key thing to remember is that you must swing the club very slowly and fully. Concentrate on a very slow, fluid movement. It is also a great way to in-grain better positioning of the club. Remember that you're swinging a super-heavy club. Trying to swing it at anything like normal speed could lead to injury. Hold each key checkpoint position for fifteen seconds. After just a fifteen-second hold you will be surprised by the effort.

As you slowly move the club into the backswing, you'll feel the weight of the clubhead and clubshaft working on your forearms. Later, after your arms have passed waist height and the clubshaft has passed perpendicular, you'll actually feel it begin to pull on your hips, back, and shoulders, so that they'll want to keep turning ever farther. For anyone looking for more coil, or a longer back-swing, the weight of your training club will encourage you to stretch your body and go beyond your existing at-the-top position. Don't try to decide in advance how much farther you want to swing back than normal. Just let the training club do its work. Then, very slowly and smoothly, start the clubshaft back down, around, and through the impact zone and into the finish.

Start slowly with your weighted-club training, ideally with my *McLean Power System* (call 1-800-847-9464 or visit *www.swingrite2.com*) that includes specially designed weighted clubs. I recommend you make about a dozen slow swings a day the first week or so. Then add a few more slow swings per day the second week, and a few more the next, until you're making about twenty or more swings a day. You'll find that, over time, that weight at the top of the backswing will pull you around a little farther and a little farther. If you continue this exercise over, say, two months, you just won't believe how much turn you'll have added to your backswing, and how much stronger your muscles have become.

The accompanying photograph shows me working out the Jim McLean Release Club; it weighs 3.5 pounds and has a bend in the shaft for training you to create and employ a proper and powerful release action. The other two specially designed weighted clubs are resting on the small practice bag.

I also love the weighted clubs for improving swing positions. Hold the critical positions you need to upgrade for twenty seconds, then repeat. Vijay Singh uses the weighted club daily. I know it has done wonders for his game. We have talked about the heavy club many times on the range at Doral. I've greatly enjoyed watching Vijay work on numerous swing positions with his weighted clubs.

DRIVING INSTRUCTIONS FOR ADVANCED GOLFERS

Chapter 1

TRUE TEST-DRIVING

In talking to advanced players who visit me at the Doral Resort in Miami, Florida, and my other schools around the country, I find that they are very knowledgeable about what's hot in driver technology. The average advanced player knows all about graphite shafts, steel shafts, kick-points, shaft flexes, head-size advantages and disadvantages, loft, lie, and, of course, the importance of aesthetic appeal in a driver. All the same, while the tour pro keeps looking and testing out new drivers even when he's hitting the ball well, many advanced players operate according to the "If it ain't broke, don't fix it" philosophy. Therefore, they fail to improve their driving prowess as much as they might otherwise.

By spending time periodically with a local club-fitting expert, or experimenting with new drivers during demonstration or "demo" days at your local club, you just may find a new driver that will allow you to hit the ball even farther and straighter with less physical effort.

When testing out new drivers, be adventurous and cast your ego aside. Don't be embarrassed to try a higher-lofted driver or one with a regular shaft if you're not as strong and flexible as you once were and lack the luxury of being able to devote hours to practice as in days past.

You might be surprised by the results with a new driver. And because golf is a game of inches, a club that hits the ball just a few yards longer or a few degrees straighter might make a significant difference in your scoring and allow you to attain a better level of play.

Chapter 2

HOW TO HIT A CONTROLLED, SUPER-POWERFUL FADE

There's a chance that you already play a power-fade shot off the tee and a soft cut on fairway shots into the green. I say this, knowing that many advanced golfers are control players. So I'd be willing to bet that you know that the fade is the perfect play on dogleg holes that curve right, ideal when hitting to firm, undulating fairways bordered by trouble, and a super shot to play into a left-to-right crosswind when you're looking to ride the wind, or into a right-to-left crosswind when you're looking to control trajectory.

The power fade has been used by many of golf's greatest drivers, including Ben Hogan, Hale Irwin, Lee Trevino, Jack Nicklaus, Vijay Singh, and Bruce Lietzke, my old college roommate at the University of Houston and the 2003 U.S. Senior Open champion. I think you'll agree that this is an impressive list of players, so you may just want to follow me to the driving range.

When setting up to play a controlled, super-powerful fade tee shot, experiment with your grip by adjusting your top hand slightly more toward the target (but just slightly, so the V formed by your thumb and forefinger points between your right ear and chin). Aim your feet, knees, hips, and shoulders left of the target (see page six of color insert, in the Driving Lessons segment for the Advanced Player), and open the clubface very slightly. The more fade-spin you want to impart to the ball, the more you should open the clubface. Some players like to tee the ball lower than normal because it promotes more of a down-and-across path that is needed for this shot, but this type of swing often produces too much spin and results in extra-high "up-shoot" shots. My recommendation is to tee the ball higher and play it off your left instep to ensure a clean upswing hit. Moving the ball forward is a major key.

On the backswing, take the club along your bodyline, and brace and resist your lower body. To enhance control, limit your backswing turn.

Coming down, shift your hips toward the target before clearing them to the left. The downswing trigger is the lateral shift. In fact, once you reach the top of the swing, you should follow the example set by the great Ben Hogan, arguably the best ball-striker of all time.

In 1969, while I was playing for the University of Houston golf team, a friend of mine called to tell me that Hogan was going to play Champions Country Club in Houston, Texas. I was on the road in a New York minute. This was a shot-making and learning exhibition I did not want to miss.

Watching Hogan hit shots was educational. Six or seven times, the few others who had received a tip on the hottest ticket in town and I stared in awe as Hogan played one masterful shot after another at Champions. I was very fortunate to get this opportunity to watch Hogan play rounds with such pros as Jack Burke, Jr., John Mahaffey, Jay Herbert, and Jimmy Burke.

It's hard to single out one solitary secret. However, I'm sure that one of the strongest elements of Hogan's swing was the way he moved his hips. The "Hawk" fired them so fast that I only noticed a flash. It is an idea that Bruce Lietzke has used for his entire career, although I believe he shifts his hips even more laterally than Hogan did. Bruce was named the number-one driver on the PGA Tour nine times, so it's obvious that his hip-slide helps him hit controlled power-fade shots onto fairway after fairway from the tee.

Shifting the hips laterally triggers the transfer of weight from your right side to your left side and, more importantly, automatically drops your hands, arms, and the club down into the perfect hitting slot, or what I call the "attack track."

The true secret to executing the power fade was taught to me many years ago by the legendary pro golfer Gene Sarazen, in Marco Island, Florida. Gene used what he called a "knuckle-up" release action to ensure a left-to-right tee shot.

In the hitting area, the key is releasing the left hand under through impact. This "under-release" promotes a powerful strike of club to ball, rather than a hang-on, weak, block-cut shot. Modern players like Vijay Singh, Fred Couples, and Phil Mickelson are great examples of players who use Sarazen's move.

The result is a shot that flies powerfully off the clubface, rises quickly, and levels off into a penetrating trajectory as it fades back to your final target in the center of the fairway. The power fade will also roll a good distance, and that is usually a surprise to even an advanced golfer.

Here I am physically rehearsing Gene Sarazen's release-action secret, before I hit balls. You should follow the same practice procedure. Feel the move first.

Chapter 3

THE POWER LINE: THE KEY SECRET LINK TO HITTING BULLET-LIKE DRIVES

Although legendary golfers Ben Hogan, Jack Nicklaus, and Lee Trevino preferred to hit the power fade, they had a neutral to slight fade path. If there is a single secret to ball striking, this is it. The geometry and arc of your golf swing, starting down and through impact, is vitally important, and the key to hitting bullet-straight drives.

I started observing film with Carl Welty to try to determine the secret of consistent driving. What I discovered was what I named the Power Line.

Two corners of the swing form the Power Line: the delivery position and the release. Between the two, the clubhead follows a powerful arc through impact. In the ideal delivery position, the shaft of the club is parallel to the target line. This indicates that the club is on-plane, a must for straight and solid ball-striking. From this position, the clubhead is released via the rotation of the hands, wrists, arms, shoulders, and torso in the proper sequence. When they all work together, you will maximize your power potential and be on your way to hitting that dead-straight bullet drive. Anyone who thinks the legs and torso do not provide tremendous power has no idea what I'm describing.

The Power Line position on the release occurs just before the club reaches horizontal. Here, the shaft again is parallel to the target line. In the ideal release, the shaft lines up with the right arm, which stays extended to create width on the follow-through. The wrists are angled down, but fully released. This is the position in the swing where you can tell if your action is connected—that is, if your body, arms, and club all are working together. All great drivers create this power release. In addition to studying the accompanying photographs showing key power-line moves, right-handed players should observe Vijay Singh (and you left-handed golfers Phil Mickelson), so that you can see how these moves come together.

Precautionary Measures: Three Ways To Lose Your Power Line

1. You start your downswing with your shoulders or uncock your wrists too early. Result: an outside delivery position, a common cause of slices and pulls.

2. Your right shoulder gets too low on the downswing and the club gets trapped behind you. Result: you have to flip your hands to try to square the clubface, a recipe for inconsistency.

3. Your right elbow gets stuck behind your right hip. From there you have to throw the elbow out away from your body. Result: power is drained from your swing.

Method teachers often like to focus tremendous time and effort on the so-called "perfect backswing." They might have a secret setup or perfect position at the top. Some researchers have compiled a composite of hundreds of tour players into a "perfect model swing." They then teach every student the exact same moves.

Opinions are fine and a big part of golf. That is because different ideas do work. Yet for me, as an instructor and owner of a major golf school, I cannot teach opinions. I have to make sure our students get better at golf. I cannot teach in a rigid method that might work well for only twenty percent of the people attending our school.

There are not many absolutes in golf, and almost nobody knows a "true" golf fundamental. The power line is a ball-striking fundamental. It has not been explored or understood by many, but I believe this chapter is the key one in the book. Understand the power line and you will begin to understand why so many different backswings work, and how swings that look so different can hit great golf shots. You will see how two players working with opposite swing theories can both play well—they both consciously, or more likely unconsciously, have a great power line move.

Chapter 4

PRO-STANDARD STRATEGIES

All low-handicap golfers have worked hard to become very good at the game. Nevertheless, if you are anything like the other top-end players I've met and talked to, your real goal is to get down to scratch (0 handicap). So I'm going to tell you what I tell them: *Don't just spend all your time working on your swing. Save some time for thinking out and applying good driving strategies.*

As hard as golf legends Jack Nicklaus and Ben Hogan worked on their driver swings, they realized early on, with help from such great teachers as Jack Grout and Henry Picard, that in order to save strokes they had to limit mental mistakes when driving the ball. The fact that both Hogan and Nicklaus learned great driving techniques is just another reason why no golfer could beat either of these two giants when they were at their best.

Ironically, something that's been kept quiet is that Hogan and Nicklaus played a number of practice rounds together, mostly before the major championships, according to the famous golf writer Herbert Warren Wind. Surely Hogan, being older, probably taught Nicklaus many things, yet Nicklaus could have taught Hogan some things, too, considering his great golf instincts and golf mind.

For the benefit of all you advanced players who know deep down that you need some work in the driving-strategy department, I'd like to reveal secrets I have learned from observing both Hogan and Nicklaus.

Legendary Driving Strategies: What Was So Special About Ben Hogan During His Heyday?

1. Hogan's strategic preparation included driving to the golf course extra slowly, to put himself in a relaxed mood, and refraining from coffee before a round, for fear that drinking caffeine would speed up his swing tempo and interfere with his strategic thought process.

2. Hogan liked to dress sharply and immaculately in conservative colors, because it made him feel more confident.

3. Hogan used a heavy, low-lofted deep-faced driver with a thick grip to help promote the fade actions he was known for. (A bigger grip promotes less hand action.) The driver might not have worked for anyone but Hogan. Yet, he found the perfect driver for his swing.

4. Hogan employed extra practice swings on the first tee—three or four to be precise—to gear his brain for his first tee shot, which he believed set the tone for the entire round.

5. Hogan depended most on the fade, the ultimate control shot, but on sharp dogleg left holes, he hit a draw to give himself an advantage on the approach. It's an advantage if you know how to hit both shots to be a great scoring strategist.

6. Hogan always had a chess-like view of the game. He used his driver to get to Point A and then he took it from there. He had a precise driving plan for each tee shot.

7. Before the round, Hogan practiced fading the ball down the left side of the range.

8. After a round, Hogan sometimes waited until he was fatigued to practice hitting drives, just so he would know what adjustments to make to his

driver setup and swing if he came down the stretch of a major championship and felt tired.

9. Hogan, like Nicklaus, never started the swing until he saw himself hit the ideal drive in his mind's eye.

Legendary Driving Strategies:
What Was So Great About Jack Nicklaus During His Heyday?

1. On the lesson tee with Jack Grout prior to a major championship round, Nicklaus practiced the shape of drive (hard fade, soft draw, etc.) that he would have to hit out on the course.

2. Nicklaus played with a slightly shorter (forty-two and three-quarter inches) but heavy, counterbalanced driver for more control.

3. Even when Nicklaus was not playing his best, he conjured up confidence, knowing that a positive attitude relaxes the body and, in turn, allows the swing to flow smoothly with acceleration.

4. Nicklaus, being very target-oriented, always picked out a specific landing area on the side of the fairway that left him the best angle to hit an attacking approach from.

5. Even though Nicklaus swung hard, he swung rhythmically, understanding the importance of maintaining balance.

6. Nicklaus placed extra importance on the opening tee shot and arrived at the first tee a little early to prepare more thoroughly than his contemporaries.

7. During the 1960s and '70s particularly, Nicklaus did not just hit a drive and quickly pick up his tee. He paused to watch the ball flight and roll of the ball to gain feedback on what he was doing right—or wrong. (See page 6 of the color insert, in the Driving Lessons segment for the Advanced Player.)

Chapter 5

IMPROVING SWING TEMPO, TIMING, AND RHYTHM

Overall, as an advanced player, your swing is good, but surely you occasionally fall into a slump. Don't panic. Even the game's greatest players start hitting off-line drives, owing to problems with the tempo, timing, and rhythm of their swing.

The tendency of most good players is to sometimes start snatching the club back too quickly or to pull it down into the ball. Both of these faults cause an overly quick tempo.

One piece of advice I can give you to help swing at a smooth, accelerating tempo comes from John Andrisani, the former senior editor of instruction at *GOLF Magazine*, who learned this tip from Sandy Lyle, at a time when Lyle was ranked number one in the world and he had won the Masters and British Open.

Lyle told Andrisani that in order to swing at a controlled tempo and gradually build acceleration, he thought of the swing as a range of tones. In other words, if your tempo is a song, the speed of your swing builds up steadily, just as a singer's voice gets higher and higher as it goes through the musical scale. Carry this image with you to the practice tee and golf course, and the tempo of your swing will improve.

When the timing of your swing is off, typically the lower body outraces the golf club. Specifically, the hips tend to clear too fast, the club lags too far behind, and you come into impact with the clubface open, or, sensing that, you whip your right hand and right forearm over, close the clubface, and hit a duck hook.

If I have just cited your problem, slow your right-leg motion. Feel a heavy right leg and incorporate a very small lateral lower-body shift into your downswing, to give your hands, arms, and the club a chance to catch up. That way, the downswing will be coordinated (body and club in time with each other) and you will hit powerfully accurate drives. To regain your timing, many times you will want to quiet your body and key on your arms falling on the down-swing.

When addressing rhythm, you can swing as fast as Sergio Garcia or as slow as Ernie Els, as long as you stay balanced and consistently return the clubface squarely to the ball with speed in the impact zone. Hit drives using swings of varying tempo, and watch your ball flight. As long as the ball shoots off the club-face and flies accurately, your tempo and timing are okay. However, if you start hitting off-line drives, gear back a notch so that your rhythm is smooth. Pick a speed or tempo of swing that is easily manageable. Surprisingly, a slightly faster tempo makes it easier to maintain good timing and rhythm, especially under pressure. I know this is the opposite of what golfers believe, but it's true. A slow

When starting the club back, it's better to employ an "up-beat" tempo of swing than a "down-beat" action. A very slow takeaway can disrupt the timing and rhythm of your swing. Staying smooth is what's important.

tempo is dangerous. For example, a super-slow backswing can lead to a quick and jerky downswing that's pretty hard to repeat. It's like hitting a bongo drum. You hit the drum to a quick beat and it's easy to repeat. Slow it down and the repeat-tempo is more difficult to replicate. There is tempo to both the backswing and downswing. We want speed, but we must maintain good timing and tempo to attain controlled speed—the priority of every top driver of the golf ball.

Chapter 6

MORE LESSONS FROM GOLF'S GREATEST DRIVERS

Throughout golf history, there have been great drivers of the golf ball, and it's no coincidence that these players are also the ones that have captured the most major championships. Golf's four majors, the Masters, U.S. Open, PGA Championship, and British Open, are always played on difficult courses that put a premium on ball placement off the tee.

Hale Irwin, a three-time U.S. Open champion, is one of these. Hale has played a fade all his golfing life, and though not long off the tee, is extremely accurate. I would also put Lee Trevino in this category. "Super Mex" won the U.S. Open twice, the PGA twice, and the British Open, owing largely to his uncanny ability to hit a low, controlled fade.

Ben Hogan and Jack Nicklaus won twenty-seven major championships between them, thanks to a controlled driving game. The fade was also their bread-and-butter shot, and both men hit the ball real long when they wanted to, especially Nicklaus.

In the category of power, I can't help talking about John Daly, Tiger Woods, and Phil Mickelson, all major championship winners. Tiger hit many controlled fade drives during his super-hot run between 1999 and 2001.

When it comes to combining power and accuracy, two-time British Open champion Greg Norman, who was ranked number one in the world for many years, and multiple major-championship winner Sam Snead are also right at the top of the list. Norman depended on a controlled fade or a straight shot, while Snead hit both fades and draws.

I'll point out some qualities of the swings of these players to explain why they were such great drivers of the ball, so that you can learn from their example.

One of Hale Irwin's assets throughout his career has been his grip. His beautiful overlap grip allows him to consistently swing on a neutral path and hit a super-accurate controlled fade.

Hogan seemed to do everything right, as I have already mentioned earlier in this book. However, if there is one thing that set him apart from other great swingers, it was his work ethic. Hogan's swing was very fast, but he made it work wonders by grooving each and every coordinated action and mechanical nuance through hard practice, much like superb driver and control player Lee Trevino. Both of these players experimented and worked things out on their own.

Then there is Nicklaus, who we also reviewed earlier. Nicklaus was the greatest driver under pressure who ever lived, and this had a lot to do with his preparation. He stuck to a pre-swing routine and never wavered from his shot-making plan. That included lining up to an interim short target and visualizing the perfect drive. He also knew he could rely on that consistent fade which effectively eliminated the left side of the golf course.

John Daly, Tiger Woods, and Phil Mickelson are all fun to watch because they love hitting the ball hard. When at their best, it's like they're hitting balls at the driving range with a totally carefree attitude. There's an important lesson to be learned here about attitude, particularly if you sometimes find yourself trying to steer the ball. Don't try too hard to control the ball. Let go mentally, and let your arms and body swing the club with maximum acceleration.

Greg Norman learned his golf mostly from his mother and from reading *Golf My Way* by Jack Nicklaus. Using the ideas laid out by Nicklaus, Norman became a great player himself and actually competed head-to-head with his golf idol. One road to improvement is knowledge. Certainly Norman benefited from the writing of Jack Nicklaus.

Sam Snead was a golfing phenomenon. You could argue that Snead's greatest asset was his footwork. His left heel lifted on the backswing and was replanted as a trigger on the downswing. I talked many hours with Sam, and he always emphasized using his feet for feel and power. Sam pushed off the instep of the right foot at the start of the downswing when he wanted to add speed to his swing. Playing barefoot as a youngster let Sam also feel how the weight should shift in order to achieve good balance, an aspect of the swing all golfers need to work on.

One of my main mentors, Ken Venturi, was also a tremendous driver of the golf ball. Ken hit the ball very accurately, too, mainly due to well-timed, consistent forearm rotation through impact. Kenny was a huge Hogan fan and played hundreds of rounds with him. When I played and worked with Venturi, he gave me fabulous information on driving. Venturi, like Hogan, played the fade.

By studying the best, you simply have to learn excellent ideas and concepts. Throughout the book, I try to bring you important details I've gleaned in my research.

Chapter 7

POST-ROUND PRACTICAL PRACTICE

If you attend a professional tour event, you will discover that many of the players return to the range after the round. So should you, since this is often the most productive time to work on your swing. After your round, you can immediately attend to shots that caused you problems. If that's the case, approach your swing faults in the way a mechanic looks at the symptoms of a poorly running car: patiently and, if necessary, with the help of another mechanic. That means your golf instructor.

After a good round of golf, you can return to the range to further groove that swing action and lock down key swing thoughts.

As strong a case as I make for post-round practice, make sure you are feeling strong enough, not fatigued physically or mentally. Frankly, if you do not feel up to added practice, you are better off saving any analytical notes you made, either mentally or physically, and applying them the next day when you're fresh and ready to work out on the driving range. Trying to work out a swing problem when you're fatigued just doesn't cut it. Frankly, it's a waste of time and, moreover, it can cause you to experiment too much and compound any minor problem or fault in your swing technique.

Say you are re-warmed up and ready to practice, and you want to figure out what caused you to hit some drives off-line during the round. Rather than assuming there's a major fault in your actual swing, first check the basics like your grip and address position. This is what the pros do, knowing that in golf all it takes is a minor setup fault to play havoc with your ability to swing on-plane and hit on-target shots. For example, an overly strong left hand grip could be the cause of your bad tee shots. Setting up with your weight favoring your toes can lead to an overly steep plane, causing sliced drives and fat irons. Setting up with too much weight on your heels can cause you to swing on an overly flat plane and hit garden-variety off-line drives.

Next, hit some short wedge shots to slow down your swing tempo. Snead liked to hit twenty or thirty seven-iron shots before moving on to the driver. If Sam swung the club poorly on the course he would hit 100 to 150 seven-iron shots during a post-round practice session to return to good form. It could just be that your swing speed was too quick out on the course and, as a result, you were throwing off your timing and rhythm.

Another mistake that good players make involves alignment. If you played a high number of dogleg right holes during the round that required you to aim left or set up open, you may have slipped into this setup and used it unknowingly on other narrow, dead-straight holes and ended up hitting the ball into the right rough. As a result, you thought you had a swing problem, when in fact you

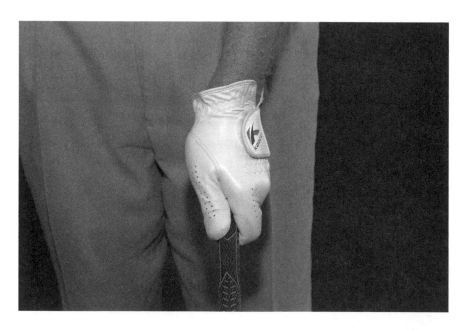

During your post-round practice, first check the "basics," like your grip, before immediately thinking you have a swing problem. You'd be surprised how a small element of your setup, like an overly strong left hand grip, may be causing your off-line shots.

had an alignment problem. Alignment mistakes are very common, so lay down several clubs to create a solid practice station.

You must understand by now what I'm trying to convey. Many times golfers make the mistake of automatically tinkering with their swing, seeking mechanical perfection, instead of working on the perfect setup or regaining certain lost "feels" related to the backswing and downswing. Once you reestablish a solid setup and/or regain those feels, you will be on the way to repeating a good swing and hitting good drives.

Another important consideration when practicing is weather. Most tour pros avoid practicing into a strong headwind, because they believe it can cause them to move the ball well back in their stance and swing too hard. They do not want to groove such a setup and swing—and neither should you. No professional likes to practice straight downwind shots. It takes curve off the ball and the shots carry too far. Ideally, when practicing driving, you want there to be no wind. However, a moderate or right-to-left wind is okay, too.

When working on your driver swing, it's also a good idea to mix up your shots, hitting a few fades first and then some draws. Jack Nicklaus used to do this when he was winning on tour, claiming that it reduced the possibility of exaggerating any one aspect of his swing, piqued his interest, presented a special challenge, and was instructional because it taught him what causes what results in the golf swing.

I realize that unlike the top tour pros, who often have their coaches on hand at tournaments to help them, you're probably all alone on the practice tee. Understandably, you often get stumped as to what's wrong with your game. If after checking the basics for the driver setup you fail to find anything wrong, you should always analyze your ball flight. The push-shot that you hit on the course may have been caused by swinging the club on too flat a plane, while the pull-shot can often be traced to an outside-inside swing path. The slice you hit can be traced to swinging across the target line with the clubface open at impact. The pull hook can be caused by swinging across the target line with the clubface closed. Golf is truly a game of adjustments, and nobody has driving down perfect all year.

In the end, if you can't figure out what's wrong and your golf professional is not available, have some videotape taken of your swing and then return to the quiet of your home and study it. Ideally, you should have some old footage showing your good swings, which makes it easier to pick out new flaws when you compare them.

As you might guess, I highly recommend you try video if you're an experienced player looking to improve. But make sure you have a trained, respected teacher diagnose the problem areas first. What's more, be certain that you are taped from the exact same angles and from the same distance, because even minor moves of the camera will change everything you see. I'm fanatical about camera angles, and it's a big reason why I'm able to do such solid research on the golf swing.

PART II

WEDGE WISDOM

Depending on a player's handicap, the wedge—be it a pitching wedge, gap-wedge, sand wedge, or lob wedge—plays different roles.

For a Beginner golfer, being a good wedge player is like having a life preserver when you're stranded at sea. The wedge helps a player save par or bogey when he hits an approach shot that lands well left or right of the green. But that's not to say that the wedge should be perceived solely as a bailout club.

Mid-Level players, who might be short and accurate off the tee, depend on the wedge to hit their third shots close to the hole on long par-fours.

The wedge is also the club that allows the low-handicap Advanced golfer to hit second shots close to the hole on short par-fours, tee shots stiff to the flagstick on some very short par-three holes, or approach shots on long par-fives when he or she needs to knock the ball in close to set up a birdie putt.

In this part of *The 3 Scoring Clubs*, I will focus on pitching basics for beginner golfers, wide-ranging tips that will allow a mid-level golfer to improve rapidly, and all kinds of shot-making secrets that advanced golfers need to raise their standard of wedge play. Everything from how to think, how to practice, and how to hit the ball close whether you're 120 yards out or twenty feet from the hole is contained in the chapters that follow. Although the instruction differs according to what level player I'm addressing, don't think for a second that I would discourage any beginner or mid-level players from trying something daring that's normally designed for advanced players. As for advanced players, I expect that you can't wait to take on the challenge of getting your teeth into some scratch-level tips and trying to take your own wedge game up a notch.

So let's proceed with the lessons.

WEDGE PLAY FOR BEGINNER GOLFERS

Chapter 1

CHOOSING THE RIGHT WEDGES

Compared to the driver and putter, the pitching wedge does not get the credit it deserves from beginner golfers, even though they use it so often during a round of golf. The same goes for any other sand wedge of any loft that you might carry.

To appreciate how underrated the wedge game is, all you have to do is sit around the 19th hole and listen to the other golfers in the room. They will talk about how far they hit a drive on a particular hole or how many putts they sank. But rarely, unless a low-handicap player is talking, will you ever hear a player tell a story about how he or she hit a pitching wedge close to the hole.

Trust me, Ben Hogan and Harvey Penick would never have included the wedge as one of the three most important scoring clubs if it weren't just that. Good wedge players like Tom Kite and Justin Leonard laugh all the way to the winner's circle, knowing that this club is the one that allows them to score birdies on short par-four holes, save par on long par-fours, and score birdies on par-five holes. Where you're concerned, it will be one of the most important clubs in your bag, if you give it a chance to work for you by learning how to use it to hit various shots. But first you must choose the right pitching wedge—and for that matter, the correct sand wedge and lob wedge.

Numerous tour pros now carry four wedges: a 48-degree pitching wedge, 52-degree gap-wedge, a 56-degree sand wedge, and a 60-degree lob wedge. Others still carry three wedges: a 48-degree pitching wedge, a 53-degree sand wedge, and a 58-degree lob wedge. I do think you should change your thinking and get away from the standard two-wedge set that features just the "P.W." and "S.W." Instead, add an "L.W."—or lob wedge—and space out your lofts as I just demonstrated in the pro example: pitching wedge, 48 degrees; gap wedge, 52

Many PGA Tour professionals carry four wedges in their bag. I recommend you add at least a lob wedge to your standard pitching wedge/sand wedge set.

degrees; sand wedge, 57 degrees. All should have bounce built in. More on this is upcoming.

Carrying three wedges and spacing out the loft between them will allow you to quickly become a more versatile and exacting wedge player and save par or score birdie.

Having the right wedge in your bag can make greenside play a whole lot easier and generally improve your level of play. And I don't mean just on bunker shots. The right sand wedge can really be an asset on pitches and chips, too.

The difference between the design of the sand wedge and that of the pitching wedge and lob wedge involves much more than just loft. The most obvious difference can be seen in the design of the flange on the sand wedge. It is broader and thicker than the flange on the pitching wedge, which helps the club get through the sand on bunker shots.

But the most unique and important feature of the sand wedge is the amount of "bounce" built into the flange. Bounce refers to the degree to which the back or rear edge of the flange lies above the leading edge of the flange when the clubshaft is held in a perfectly vertical position. The sand wedge has the most bounce built into the flange. Without this bounce, the leading edge would dig too deeply into the sand behind the ball, and you certainly don't want that to happen, so check your wedges carefully.

All sand wedges are made with wider or narrower soles and greater or lesser degrees of bounce. You should select a sand wedge based on the type of sand that predominates on the course or courses you play most often. If your course has deep, soft, heavy sand, you'll find that a large-flanged club with lots of bounce (between twelve and fourteen degrees) will ride nicely through the sand and make your recoveries much simpler.

You must be very careful if the sand is shallower and firm. If the sand is thin or firm, a large-flanged club with lots of bounce will not get under the ball; it will bounce right off the base of the sand and hit the ball, and the shot will end up flying over the green. If this is the type of sand at your home course, go for a more compact blade that features a narrower sole and a couple of degrees less bounce, say six to ten degrees. Where the thin blade of the pitching wedge will allow you to nip the ball off most fairways, the sand wedge bounce will allow you to slide the club through the sand or hit off a super-tight lie in the fairway without digging down to China. One of the worst shots in golf is "laying the sod over the ball." That term refers to a deep divot hit behind the ball. A wedge with no bounce encourages this nightmare shot.

The lob wedge feature that sets it apart is loft. The lob wedge is basically designed to pop the ball out of heavy greenside rough, although many tour players and experienced golfers use this club to hit a variety of chips and pitches, and often use it for all greenside bunker shots. PGA teacher Stan Utley is a big advocate of using the lob wedge to hit bunker shots.

Former U.S. Open champion Tom Kite shared another secret with me about lob-wedge play when we worked together extensively before his 1992 U.S. Open win. This could be a huge plus in your wedge game.

Tom believes that playing with a lob wedge that is around thirty-three and a half inches in length—a full one and a half inches shorter than standard—will enhance your control. Tom realized this as early as the 1990s, so he was way ahead of everyone else. No wonder he could stand right over a wedge and be so accurate with his shots. You may want to try the same strategy by having your pro cut your lob wedge down.

Chapter 2
THE BASIC WEDGE SETUP

To play the basic pitch from the fairway, take a narrow stance, spreading your feet about ten inches apart from heel to heel and consider dropping your left foot back a few inches farther from the target line than your right. To complete

The basic pitching wedge setup: down-target view *(left)* and front view *(right).*

the pitching wedge address, be sure the ball is played near the midpoint of your stance, and that around sixty percent of your weight is on your left foot.

I advocate this setup because I learned it from the best players; I certainly did not invent it. The reasons this address position works so well can be summarized as follows: It centers you over the ball; it restricts your turn away; it provides better vision; and it helps you make consistent contact. Since you do not need power for this shot, the smaller stance promotes a more controlled swing.

Chapter 3

THE BASIC WEDGE BACKSWING

For all wedge shots, you are positioned to make a very different swing than you did for the driver. On drives, we set up to swing the club on a flatter and shallower plane, plus we seek width on the backswing to gain power. The driver is your longest and lightest club, while the wedges are the shortest and heaviest in your set of four-teen. When hitting the basic wedge shot, you set up to swing on a more upright plane, and you narrow the backswing arc to ensure a de-scending hit at impact. This sharp club-to-ball contact is what allows you to impart stop-spin on the ball.

When employing the wedge-backswing, shift only a minimum amount of weight onto your right foot and leg.

To put yourself in position to make the de-sired contact with the ball, it's critical that you shift only a minimal amount of weight onto your right foot and leg on the backswing. In fact, some of the great wedge players make no shift at all. The backswing will have turn in the shoul-ders, less in the hips, but don't simply pick up or lift the arms.

When swinging back, you must also allow your wrists to hinge, so that the hands and arms move upward into a position where you can bring the club down on the proper angle.

Chapter 4

THE BASIC WEDGE DOWNSWING

Any forced conscious effort to hit down could cause you to throw the timing of your downswing off and, as a result, drive the club into the turf behind the ball. Remember, you want to contact the ball first before taking a "shallow, bacon-strip-type divot," as television golf analyst Johnny Miller phrases it.

What will help you get the job done physically is to think of three key words: *Shift, Turn, Resist*, especially when you are first learning to master the downswing.

In order to set the downswing in motion, first make a slight lateral shift, and then, practically simultaneously, start rotating your hips as your hands, arms, and club drop into position. The actual mini-thrust of your lower body will be enough to increase your arm speed and allow you to accelerate the club down into the ball.

When making contact with the ball, you will feel a sense of hitting and holding back with the left wrist flat, particularly on shorter pitch shots. Keep accelerating

In swinging the wedge downward, make a lateral shift of the hips to trigger the motion, as I do here.

into the follow-through, with your belt buckle facing the target and the club pointing up at the target. As a checkpoint, make sure your divot is shallow.

In hitting the basic pitching wedge shot, you should still take a shallow "bacon-strip"-type divot and accelerate the club into the follow-through.

Chapter 5

HOW TO PLAY THE HIGH-FLYING FORTY YARD PITCH SHOT TO ONE HUNDRED YARD SHOT

This is a great shot to hit, especially if the ball is sitting nicely in light rough, you're hitting to a tight pin, you've got to carry a bunker, land the ball as softly and quickly on the green, and need to avoid a flyer that can be caused by hitting down too sharply on the ball.

In this situation, I recommend that you play a pitching wedge or gap wedge, because the ball is already perched up. In essence, the pitching wedge or gap wedge will act like a more-lofted wedge. If the ball were not perched, I'd suggest a sand wedge since it features the proper loft and bounce for this type of lie.

When setting up to hit this lofted pitch, play the ball forward from a narrow and open stance. Position the ball between the left heel and left instep, to ensure that you get the full value of the clubface essential to producing softly hit, soft-landing shots. Grip the club lightly to promote active hand action. You might also try choking down on the club to enhance your control of the swinging clubhead.

During the backswing, leave most of your weight left and rock your left shoulder downward just like Tiger Woods does, so that you'll propel your arms and the club upward. The club should go approximately to the three-quarter position. You will form a nice "L" position between the left arm and the clubshaft.

Coming down, shift your knees toward the target. Use the knees in order to add acceleration to the swing and to enhance timing and rhythm.

You are now ideally positioned to accelerate the arms through and slide the clubface cleanly down and through the ball. However, in order to ensure that the club sends the ball flying high into the air, follow the instructions I gave to one of my students, PGA Tour player Len Mattiace, years ago: *Concentrate on rotating your right hand under your left through impact.*

In playing a short pitch from rough, you don't need a big swing, provided you let active leg action add acceleration to the shot.

Chapter 6

KEEP YOUR DISTANCES

Every shot you face is not going to be your perfect yardage. Furthermore, you should not always play a high-flying wedge with the same club. What you need to do, then, is to experiment with different clubs and keep a record of the distance you hit each one on average with a full, three-quarter, and half swing, so when you face a shot out on the course, you'll know which club and which type of swing to use.

Take your three wedges out on the golf course one evening when the course is quiet. Go to the range when it is closed and hit five balls or more with each club. Start by making full swings and pace off the yardage, then do the same with shorter swings. When pacing off each shot, make sure your strides are one full yard. Once you complete this exercise, you'll be prepared for battle on the course, just like all the top wedge players on tour. You'll be super-confident, too, knowing your distance and swing lengths are under control.

I ask my students actually to tape those measured yardages onto the shaft of each wedge. It's a great reminder until you are absolutely sure.

Chapter 7

HOW TO PLAY THE LOW PITCH-AND-RUN SHOT

When playing a low pitch-and-run shot with a pitching wedge, the ball should roll more than carry or fly in the air. Understanding this will help you plan out the shot and visualize it. The fun comes from seeing how the flight and roll of the ball are affected by the club you selected, your setup, and the unique golf swing you employ. How you stand, where you play the ball in your stance, the loft of the club, the clubface position, and the arc and speed of your swing make a difference to the outcome of the shot, as you will now see.

To appreciate this technique fully, imagine that your ball is sitting in the middle of the fairway, twenty yards off the edge of the green and thirty-five yards from a hole that is cut on the top level of a two-tier green. The lie is tight, the putting surface firm and fast-running, and there's a strong wind at your back.

If you're playing downwind, a high pitch will not hold the green. The intelligent play is the pitch-and-run, so often used on links courses in Scotland but more and more on our shores, as well, since course superintendents are now manicuring fringes and leaving entranceways in front of the green instead of blocking them with bunkers.

To execute this shot, pick out a landing spot either in front of the green or on the lower level of the putting surface, so that the ball will bounce and then roll the rest of the way to the hole. This decision on where the landing spot should be depends on the speed of the green, its firmness, and the strength of the wind. If, for example, the green is extremely slow and the wind at your back is blowing at only five miles per hour, you would have to land the ball on the front of the green.

The key is to make a compact backswing while keeping the wrists quiet.

This technique will enable you to nip the ball off the tight, grassy fairway so that it flies on a low trajectory, lands, bounces, and scoots up to the hole.

When setting up to hit the pitch-and-run, position the ball opposite the central point in your stance, and put the majority of your weight on your left foot. Choke down and grip more firmly than normally to discourage any exaggerated wrist action. Stand erect to encourage a fluid arm-swing, and set your hands ahead of the ball to decrease the effective loft of the club and promote a low, running shot.

Swing the club back slightly inside the target line and up to waist height. You want some hinge in the right hand to promote feel.

On the downswing, keep your hands ahead of the clubhead so that you can pinch the ball off the turf. Some players have the feeling of dragging the ball due to the clubhead trailing the hands and staying low after impact. To further ensure a low-ball flight, remember to strive for a low follow-through by making your buzzwords *hit* and *resist*.

Two vital keys to playing a low pitch-and-run shot are setting your hands slightly ahead of the ball at address *(left)* and keeping them slightly ahead through impact *(right)*.

Chapter 8

WHAT YOU CAN LEARN FROM YOUR PITCHING DIVOTS

Mid-level and advanced players are usually good at learning from their divots; it's actually possible to read their direction and depth to trace a fault in your technique after errant shots. Here are some guidelines for tracing your faults. You will need to figure out what's wrong before applying the fixes discussed in the next chapter.

The perfect divot is shallow and square, which means that the entire bottom of the club has contacted the ground while the club is traveling straight down the target line. A great divot is one that starts straight or slightly left, which means the club has started to swing back to the inside after impact.

Bad divots include one that is toe-deep. This type indicates an exaggerated inside-out swing path with too much hand action, or that the player's club is too upright. One thing that Ken Venturi has always said is that if anything, wedges should be flatter than too upright. (You will play better golf and take more shallow divots if your wedge is perfectly suited to your physical size and natural swing tendencies, so have yours checked.)

An ugly divot is one that starts well in front of the ball's original position and points well left of target. This type of divot indicates that you came over the top and used far too much upper-body action and ended up well ahead of the ball at impact, making extremely bad contact with the ball.

Before leaving the subject of divots, let me clear up one misconception. Some golfers believe that an inside-out divot is the goal of a good player. This is absolutely false. Experienced players know that a good divot begins after contact with the ball when the golf club is ideally swinging on an arc. A divot that points well right of the target indicates a dramatic inside-out swing path. Golfers who create this type of divot in the grass are ones who hit many shots to the right of the green, or certainly well right of the hole.

Driving Lessons: The Eight-Step Backswing and Downswing

Unless you are a beginner player who is innately blessed with extraordinary feel and hand-eye coordination, you're much more likely to arrive in a good impact position *(top)* if you swing to the top of the backswing like I do here *(center)*, and look like me moving down to the ball *(bottom)*.

WEDGE WISDOM AND PUTTING LESSONS

Wrist-Action Wedge-Chips and Learning the Seesaw Putting Stroke

Incorporating some wrist action into your chip stroke, as I do here when playing a greenside wedge shot *(left)* will prevent you from making an overly tense, robotlike stroke, and will help your distance control.

Improving your putting skills might just be a matter of learning the seesaw action I teach beginner players. When practicing, let the left shoulder rock downward slightly on the backstroke *(below left)* and upward on the forward stroke *(below right)*.

DRIVING, WEDGE GAME, AND PUTTING INSTRUCTION FOR THE MID-LEVEL PLAYER

Driving Lessons: Correct Body and Pivot Actions

This is how your feet, knees, hips, shoulders, and head should move as you swing into the at-the-top position *(left)*, impact *(below left)*, and the finish *(below right)*. Rehearse without a club until you develop a good feel for the correct body actions.

WEDGE WISDOM AND PUTTING LESSONS

Sand Wedge Chips and Belly Putter Training

When facing a short shot from fringe grass, try hitting a sand wedge instead of a seven-iron, making sure to turn through the shot *(left),* and you'll like the result.

If you're a golfer who tends to manipulate the putter with your hands, hinge the wrists on the backstroke, move the head dramatically during the stroke, or chop down on the ball at impact, practicing with a long belly putter *(below)* can help you iron out your problems.

DRIVING, WEDGE GAME, AND PUTTING INSTRUCTION FOR THE ADVANCED PLAYER

Driving Lessons: Setup Secrets for Hitting the Power-Fade Tee Shot and Studying Ball Flight

To learn to hit a super-controlled Ben Hogan–type power-fade drive, create a workstation like the one here *(above)*, since it will train you to aim your body and club correctly.

To further educate yourself in the department of driving, don't be too quick to bend down and pick up your tee after hitting a tee shot. Study the flight pattern, trajectory, and roll of the ball *(below)*, like Jack Nicklaus did in his heyday. You'll be surprised what you can learn about your swing from watching good and bad shots.

WEDGE WISDOM

Experimental Practice

Becoming a wedge-game virtuoso who can look at a lie, read it, and know exactly what wedge and technique will work best requires you to be creative when practicing. That's truly the only shortcut to becoming a wedge wizard. So, instead of practicing basic wedge chips and pitches, work on more unique shots. For example, a shot over a bunker to a tight pin *(top)*, a short shot out of a bad lie *(center)*, or shot off an uphill lie *(bottom)*.

PUTTING LESSONS

The Short Follow-Through Stroke and the Benefits of Adjusting

The short follow-through putting stroke, used successfully by such major championship winners as Ben Crenshaw, Gary Player, Bobby Locke, Billy Casper, Dave Stockton, and Jack Nicklaus, promotes acceleration. Just think of hammering a nail and you'll get the idea.

To practice this stroke, do what legendary teacher Bob Toski taught me to do: putt using a shoe instead of a ball *(above)*. The shoe is hard to move, so you'll quickly groove the short follow-through stroke.

Improvising at golf, particularly putting, is all about making adjustments, as former Masters and PGA Champion Jack Burke, Jr., taught me. So don't be afraid to make changes, such as bending over more and opening your putting

Chapter 9

THE WORST WEDGE SHOTS— AND WONDERFUL REMEDIES

FAT PITCHES

If you hit the ball heavy or fat with a pitching wedge, taking out a big chunk of turf, analyze your backswing action. Often, in an attempt to swing the club back on the desired upright plane, you have failed to turn your shoulders. Instead, you've simply lifted your arms and picked the club up vertically in the air, where you are poised to drive the club deep into the ground like an ax into a log.

Remedy: Even though you're playing a pitching wedge, you still must swing the golf club on a plane. The plane for your wedge is more upright, but it is still on an angle.

Although the clubhead will not swing low to the ground for very long, it should not be picked straight up into the air. You must allow your shoulders to turn in the backswing. You don't have to make the strong degree of windup that you would for hitting a driver, but you still have to rotate your left shoulder under your chin. Doing this allows you to swing the club on the proper path and plane and generate sufficient power to propel the ball the proper distance to the hole.

When playing a wedge, even though the action is upright, you still must turn and swing on a plane, as illustrated here.

A CASE OF THE PULLS

One of the worst feelings is hitting a wedge shot dead left of target. Very often, you can set up squarely to the ball, employ an even takeaway action, turn your shoulders, shift your weight to the inside of your right leg and move into a square position to trigger the downswing, but you still yank the shot left of the green. Why? Well, one common reason for hitting this faulty shot is failing to clear your left hip and knee fully. So your head locks itself into virtually a static position. What's worse, your body stops or freezes. Your arms and hands flash past your body causing the pull. Another cause of the pull is when your right hand takes command of the downswing, your left hand can't hold the club square to the target at impact. The result of this right-hand control: the clubface closes, causing the ball to fly dead left.

One critical aspect of curing a pull problem and hitting crisp on-target wedge shots is letting your right knee release on the downswing, as mine starts to do here.

Remedy: Once you move back onto your left side in the downswing (and you should never have moved off it that much to begin with on pitch shots), allow your left hip to clear, or turn to your left. Now your right knee and right heel will release. The right knee can be a great key for controlling distance. Many great wedge players, such as Hale Irwin, use active right-knee action. It is a big thing Ken Venturi showed me about great wedge play.

When you allow your left side to clear and the right side to fire, your hand action can vary from very passive to very active for specialty shots. Quiet hands through impact create shots with less spin but a very high degree of control. This type of hand action creates shots that hit the green, bounce two times, and then stop. Fast hands produce wedge shots that hit the green and spin back.

THIN SHOTS

One chief reason why beginners hit thin wedge shots is a misunderstanding of the swing path. If you suffer from a thin, low shot that often flies right of the target, you probably have been advised somewhere along the way to swing the club from in to out. It's no surprise that, if you swing the clubhead at the ball on an inside path, you will usually catch it with the bottom of the clubface instead of the sweet spot.

Remedy: To get back on track, visualize the proper inside-square-inside swing path, particularly the club moving back to the inside through impact. Swing the club back on a more upright path. Then swing down, allowing your hips to clear and your arms to swing freely through. Visualize the body turning more level and more left. Think "Level-Left." You can also visualize the club and hands swinging left after impact. Let the swing happen.

Visualizing this inside through-impact path before you swing, then making it happen during the swing, will cure your thin-shot problem.

THE DREADED SHANK

Every golfer agrees that the shank or "socket," as the British call it, is the ugliest shot in golf. The ball shoots dead right off the clubface, usually flies low, and often lands in deep trouble.

One major cause of the shank is dropping the club too far inside with the hosel or neck of the club leading.

Remedy: At the practice tee, put a second ball directly outside the ball you will address for this drill, so there's a three-inch space between them.

Then address the ball closest to you. Swing, trying to make contact without hitting the outside ball. You'll see how fast this drill will get your swing back on track.

Here are some other tips for eliminating other types of shanks:

1. Try standing an inch or so farther from the ball at address, with your weight evenly distributed on both feet. This setup will provide you with more freedom and the added balance you need to make a pure golf swing and hit the ball squarely and solidly. Sometimes the cure is unbelievably simple.

2. Key on driving your right shoulder under your chin through impact, rather than letting it jut outward. This will prevent your weight from lurching forward on your toes during the downswing and throwing your swing path off-track.

One common cause of the shank is looping the clubhead over the top on the downswing.

3. Most amateurs shank shots because they roll the clubshaft flat on the back-swing and then loop the clubhead over the top on the downswing. This out-to-in swing throws the clubhead just enough outside to hit the hosel every time. You cure this problem by setting the wrists so the clubshaft is almost vertical at step three of my Eight-Step Swing. I also put a shoebox, head-cover, or board about two inches outside the ball. The more up-and-down motion of the club ensures that you never get the club outside the target line.

To cure an over-the-top shank problem, hit shots with a shoebox or head-cover outside the ball, since it's safer than the board I use here and other times in practice to really discipline myself on swinging correctly. This drill will encourage you to swing on the correct path.

Chapter 10

CHOOSING BETWEEN TWO CLASSIC CHIPPING METHODS

During a round of eighteen holes, there will be some chips I would prefer to hit with dead hands and wrists. Basically, that means you swing in a pendulum fashion, using your arms and shoulders to control the action and let the natural loft of the club lift the ball and then roll it like a putt. Generally, the dead-handed method is used to play a chip off a good lie, either with a wedge or a rescue-type utility club to a very hard or very fast surface. This type of chipping technique produces a shot that lands with very little spin and is thus very easy to control on a consistent basis. It's a technique that prevents the base from getting away from you too fast.

Because of the uneven, un-manicured terrain outside the green's immediate fringe area, you will often have to add or decrease loft to the club. That's accomplished by leaning your weight left and hitting down sharply, or conversely moving the ball forward and hitting on a more level approach, so that you basically pick the ball off the turf at the bottom of the swing's arc.

For most chip shots, I prefer some wrist action (see page three of color insert, in the Wedge Wisdom segment for the Beginner Player), and I recommend that you first learn how to master this basic swing technique before you move on to developing a more refined repertoire of shots. Let me explain my philosophy.

Begin by understanding that you have to practice a short game, no matter what method you choose to use as your shot-making base: incorporating hand action or depending on a dead-wristed method. The wonderful thing about practicing my basic chipping method is that it incorporates the same basics as a full golf swing. Essentially, you are practicing a small swing action that duplicates the important fundamentals of the big swing. Because it feels more natural, it is easier to learn. Keeping the hands dead quiet is important sometimes, but it is

I think you'll hit more solid chip shots *(left)* if you incorporate some wrist-hinge on the backswing *(right)*.

always a technique that feels unnatural. Besides, when you use and train your hands in a swing, you learn to control the clubface. Therefore, your feel for playing all types of delicate touch shots is heightened.

Generally, a dead-wristed chipper is much less versatile, unless he or she has hours and hours to practice and develop finely tuned hand-eye coordination. By locking the wrists, this player has to depend almost entirely on the loft of the club to hit a high or low shot, and from certain kinds of lies this technique does not always work. It makes most golfers look very robotic and it is much more difficult to develop feel.

Using wrist action will provide you with the opportunity to hit a shot higher by turning your right hand under your left through impact, or lower by rolling your right hand over and shutting the clubface slightly. In short, I believe both ways of chipping are important, though overall you will more quickly evolve into a virtuoso and reach a higher level of play if you allow your wrists to help you feel and execute a good chip shot.

Ray Floyd, considered one of the great chippers of all time, won four major championships and many PGA Tour events using a wrist-oriented chipping method. For that matter, so have almost all the other great champions. Learn to use your hands.

Chapter 11

SAND SMARTS

When playing the basic bunker shot, know that your sand wedge is on your side. That is, if you own a good one. The bounce of the club will take care of business if you allow it to.

To play this shot, open your stance and wiggle your feet into the sand so that you establish a solid base to swing from and can feel the texture of the sand. Position the ball up in your stance, from the center all the way up to your front toe. Slide your hips a bit forward toward the target. Open the face of the sand wedge by leaning the shaft just slightly away from the target or by fanning the clubface into a more lofted position. Relax your neck, shoulders, arm and wrist muscles, lighten your grip, and make sure about sixty percent of your weight is on your left foot.

The most important thing on the backswing is swinging the club up freely by letting the wrists hinge freely, just as the great Claude Harmon, Sr., the 1948 Masters champion and, I believe, the greatest bunker-play teacher, showed me. Once you swing back to the top, making a strong shoulder turn for power, swing the club down in front of you, and slap the sand with the bounce of the club in an area three to four inches behind the ball. Experimental practice will tell you how many inches you should strike the sand behind the ball, but as Claude proved to me, it will be around three to four inches, instead of the one to two inches that golfers generally strive for.

To gain speed and propel the ball the proper distance, make sure to release the right arm freely. You are actually trying to have the clubhead get out in front of the hands prior to impact.

I've talked with Claude Harmon, Sr., many times about right-hand-controlled bunker play, as well as with accomplished sand players Ken Venturi and Johnny Revolta, all of whom advocated this method. I'm convinced it's the best. I'm pretty sure that it was Johnny Revolta who first showed Claude the basics of the sand shot. Then Mr. Harmon improved upon them. Revolta, Harmon, and Venturi all lived in Palm Springs, California, for many winters.

Here's some reminder pointers, based on what the aforementioned golf geniuses taught me.

Keep your weight on your left side, swing the club sharply upward with your right hand, cocking the wrist much earlier than you would for your normal fairway shots. At the top, you'll want the left wrist to be in a cupped position. This means the clubface will also be very open.

Your priority on the downswing is to snap the clubhead downward with an early release motion of the right hand. Be aggressive: Spank the sand. Do one more thing that Harmon taught me, and that I teach my students today: Practice bunker shots using just your right hand.

Practicing sand shots the Claude Harmon, Sr., way—with your right hand only—will help you quickly evolve into a superb bunker player. What's most important is allowing your right arm to release freely, as demonstrated here.

Chapter 12

CREATIVE PRACTICE

The greatest reward for practicing your wedge game is being able to bring new skills to the course and save shots. If you practice properly, you'll be able to look at a lie and immediately figure out the best wedge to play, how the grass will affect spin, how hard to swing, and how the ball will react once it hits the green.

All this takes time, because you must graduate from one level to the next. However, to earn a good grade here, I want you to do just one thing: Hit low punch wedge shots to learn the feel of the descending blow needed to hit the most commonly played basic pitch we reviewed in Chapters 2, 3, and 4.

When practicing, play the ball back slightly in your stance with your hands just barely ahead of the club at address. Cock the wrists fully on your backswing and practice hitting down on the ball. This simple exercise will encourage the sharp clubface-to-ball contact you'll need to hit.

WEDGE-PLAY INSTRUCTIONS FOR MID-LEVEL GOLFERS

Chapter 1
CHIPPING OPTIONS

Hitting good short shots is even more critical to scoring nowadays. The reason? The high number of courses being built that feature fast, undulating greens. Even the more established country clubs are giving putting surfaces a buzz cut to stay with the trend of having pro-venue-type courses for members to play on.

Two critical keys to hitting a sand wedge chip from fringe grass close to the hole are taking the club away slowly *(left)* and keeping the clubface open through impact *(right)*.

When you are a few yards off the green in the fringe grass, hitting to a pin about thirty feet away, we used to advocate a seven- or eight-iron and run-shot. Now, with much faster and firmer conditions, you are often much better off learning to master wedge-chipping, following these tips.

Select a sand wedge, play the ball in the middle of your stance, and make a short backswing, allowing your right wrist to hinge freely. On the backswing, I suggest you slow down. Many amateurs take the club away too quickly. Swing down and through the ball allowing the left elbow to soften and even slide. Keep a firm left wrist so that you "hold the angle," as we teachers say, and keep the clubface open. The ball will pop out softly, fly over hills and bumps and trickle toward the hole. One more thing: because you lock in the wrist angle and hold the face open through impact, be certain to turn through the shot (see page five of color insert, in the Wedge Wisdom segment for the Mid-Level player). Let your eyes follow the ball.

Chapter 2

TURNING HEADS

Many Beginner and Mid-Level golfers hit fat wedges and lose strokes because they concentrate too hard on keeping their head down and their eyes on the ball when playing short pitch shots.

To the contrary, many of the game's best players let their head turn with their shoulders and actually look up off the ball before impact. Jim Furyk and Annika Sorenstam are two top pros who "look off" on drives and irons, so I'm not surprised that they do this on short greenside shots, too. I was surprised, however, to notice Ernie Els, Tiger Woods, and other great short-game artists doing the same thing on pitch shots. They don't look off the ball on full swings, but they do on small shots around the green.

Why? On short shots I believe it is a great benefit to keep the hands, arms, and shoulders connected through im-

On this short shot I'm already looking at the hole and as you can see the golf ball is barely airborne. What does this prove? I let my head turn with my shoulders and I actually looked up before impact, just like major championship winners and short-game wizards Tiger Woods, Ernie Els, Jim Furyk, and Annika Sorenstam all do.

pact, or moving together. To me, it is the most important mechanical antidote to choking.

Choking is often not mental. Rather, it is a mechanical malfunction. Once you hit a string of awful shots, then—and only then—will you become a mental basket case. On short shots, the more you focus on keeping the head steady and down the worse you become, and the more fearful you'll be on upcoming pitches. Then you, and anyone else, will fear every short shot.

Over the years I have helped some unbelievably bad wedge players by having them imagine a rope secured around their body. Sometimes, I will go so far as to tie a belt around the upper arms. Now, the only way they can move the club effectively is with body rotation or pivot. They can use some hand rotation. Footwork is paramount when learning this technique. The game's best wedge players use their feet to turn the hips and shift their weight in order to employ a more rhythmic action. Power is provided mostly by the shoulders, which leads to my major point: *When the shoulders turn toward the target they take the head with them.* You might say that the head goes where the body takes it.

Here, I show you what I mean by a solid left wrist, as I mimic the impact position.

At impact, in the correct pitching motion, the shoulders are rotated left of the target line. They are not parallel to the target line as some teachers and many golfers believe. Because this is true, it is also the main reason why many of golf's great short-game experts are looking off the ball when the club makes contact with it.

Rotation makes it far easier to keep the left wrist solid at impact. It prevents flip and breakdown prior to impact. This makes it easy to have forward-lean on the golf shaft at impact. It is something we teach every day at our schools and something that every teacher under me wants to see from his students. It is far easier to control distance by rotating your shoulders and using them as a major power source. By not rotating through impact, you must depend on the small muscles of the body to time the shot just right. Under pressure, that is very tough to do.

Watch the pros carefully and you'll see what I mean. This is something nobody's talked about until now.

Chapter 3

THE LOB–WEDGE CUT TECHNIQUE

This shot is perfect when there is a hazard between the ball and the pin and you have very little green to work with. You can play this shot with a sand wedge, but I prefer a high-lofted lob wedge.

When setting up, play the ball opposite your left instep in an exaggerated open and wide stance. Place about sixty percent of your weight on your right foot and set your hands behind the ball slightly.

On the backswing, swing the lob wedge up outside the ball-hole target line, using a lazy full action.

Swing the wedge down across the ball in an outside-in fashion so that the club's heel leads its toe, all the time keeping your head and body quite steady. You don't want to have too much body action on this shot.

If the execution is correct, the club will slide under the ball, which will pop up over the hazard, land softly on the green, and trickle to the hole. Remember to allow for the cut spin.

You should think twice about using a sand wedge if you are hitting off a tight fairway because of the added bounce this club features. The club could bounce too much off the ground into the ball and cause you to hit a low, screaming "skull" shot that will run over your target area. So make sure you have enough cushion under the ball before trying this shot during a round of golf.

One of the most important keys to playing the lob-wedge cut is taking the club back outside the target line.

Chapter 4

HOW TO PLAY THE BURNING WEDGE KNOCKDOWN SHOT

Here's a technique that is ideal when hitting into a headwind and for playing low "stinger" wedges.

I learned how to play the knockdown on the windy courses of Texas, with some advice from teammates at the University of Houston. Later, I closely observed Lee Trevino and talked with him about his fantastic burning wedge shots. The control Lee had was brilliant. To hit this shot, play the ball in the middle of your stance, with slightly more weight on your left foot.

There are several major secrets to this shot. The first is to elevate your arms immediately in the backswing. Do this with very little wrist setting and not much turn either. Trevino took the club slightly outside, which I also advocate you try. You will definitely feel separation of your arms from your body. Your legs should feel as if they are stuck in cement throughout the backswing. The second secret is how you start down. Trevino noticeably

One secret to playing the burning wedge shot that I learned from Lee Trevino is to elevate the arms immediately in the backswing with very little wrist-set.

dropped his arms and increased his wrist cock. That means as you start down you allow this motion to pull your wrists back. What makes this move really work is the next secret, which is knee-drive. Trevino told me to "break the knees toward the target." Besides the aforementioned increase in wrist cock, this move also puts your weight fully into your left side, ensuring a sharp descending blow on the ball. To me it feels like you are taking the loft off the wedge and this thought works great for my students. You hit the shot with a bowed left wrist and short three-quarter finish. Your shot will burn into the green low but with massive backspin.

Chapter 5

HOW TO PLAY A SUPER-SOFT GAP WEDGE/SAND WEDGE SHOT FROM LIGHT ROUGH

When you are in the 10–90 yard range, hitting from light rough, try this shot that requires a different technique than you might be accustomed to.

Set up with the ball opposite the left heel. Next, open the clubface of your gap wedge or sand wedge to program loft into the shot.

When hitting this type of shot, you need to make a slightly more wrist-oriented, V-shaped swing. This action allows the club to enter the impact zone with less chance of getting snagged in the grass and twisting closed or open. When swinging back to the top, set the wrists early and keep the clubface square to open (never closed).

After reaching the top, lead the club through the ball with your left hand. Your left hand plays the lead role as you maintain the desired open clubface position through impact. This is a shot where you want to send the ball flying into the air quickly.

Opening the clubface is a technical "must" when setting up to play a super-soft gap or sand wedge shot from light rough.

The ball will come out high and land "dead." It is not the type of shot that will spin, so if you are hitting downwind or playing to a hard green, allow for extra roll.

The 60-degree wedge will also work for this shot, but I know many golfers do not carry one. That's when you use the technique described above.

Chapter 6

HOW TO PLAY A LONG PITCH FROM HEAVY ROUGH

When hitting a long pitch shot from high rough, play the ball back in a slightly open stance. The face of your sand wedge should be square instead of open, so you reduce the chance of undercutting the shot too much and leaving it short.

Swing the club back to the three-quarter point on an upright plane, while allowing both wrists to hinge freely. As Ken Venturi says: "There are a lot of frequencies in the wrists, and when hitting a lob from heavy rough you must maximize them to generate a good degree of club speed." According to Venturi, the hinge and then unhinge effect is a lot like drawing back a catapult and then letting go, so that at impact that club is plowing through the grass at high speed with maximum effect.

Swing down on a steep angle, keeping your left-hand grip firm to prevent the clubface from closing down in the impact zone.

Chapter 7

FUNKY LIES

In order to improve your level of play, you must know how to handle all types of lies. Here's a crash course of condensed tips to help you do just that on wedge shots.

BALL IN DIVOT

Play the ball back in your stance with your hands ahead and sixty percent of weight on your left foot. On the backswing, take the club up quite steeply. Then swing down, letting your hands lead the club into the ball. Make sure to contact the ball first.

BALL IN CUPPY LIE (MINIATURE HOLLOW IN THE GRASS)

This lie makes it difficult to get at the ball. A cut shot is advised. To accomplish this sideswipe action, swing the wedge back outside the target line. Start down by clearing your left hip quickly to the left. This will give your arms room to swing the club freely across the target line. The shot you hit will fade in the air, then spin from left to right on the green.

DOWNHILL LIE

Take one less club (i.e., a sand wedge instead of a gap wedge) to allow for the effective decrease in the club's loft at impact. Position your body parallel to the slope. Play the ball closer to your back foot. Make a compact backswing. Swing down the slope while keeping your body going forward. It is easy to hit behind the ball from this lie, so make sure to set up correctly.

UPHILL LIE

Take one more club (i.e., a pitching wedge rather than a sand wedge) to allow for the effective increase in the club's loft at impact. Position your body parallel to the slope. Play the ball in the center of your stance. Employ a controlled backswing. Swing up the slope.

HARDPAN LIE (TRODDEN-DOWN DIRT OR SAND)

Make a controlled backswing. On the way down, keep your right wrist flexed back so there's no flippiness of the clubhead through the impact zone. Hit down and through the ball. The shot will start low, rise to its apex, and then bite on the green with plenty of spin. Try to stay level going through the shot and avoid dipping down.

TIGHT LIE

When playing a pitch off this lie, particularly in the twenty-to-forty-yard range, take an open stance, position your hands behind the ball, open the clubface, and play the shot like a bunker explosion. Set up to the shot quite quickly, too, so you don't think too much and tense up. Once you swing back smoothly, concentrate on trying to slap the club into the ground first. You are trying to purposely hit a fat shot.

This particular shot is mostly for the advanced player. It will take practice and a large dose of confidence. However, I've seen many mid-level players execute this shot even in pressure situations. So you can learn it, if you work hard.

Chapter 8

SAND TIPS

Now that you are a mid-level player looking to become an advanced player, it's important that you move beyond shot-making basics and learn what to do in different conditions and situations, such as those that follow.

FIRM/WET SAND

The ball will come out faster, fly lower, and often roll farther, so allow for that by swinging slowly. As for club selection, use either a sixty-degree wedge with a minimal degree of bounce or a pitching wedge. Both clubs are less angled on the flange, and this reduces the chances of hitting a skull-shot.

SHORT BUNKER SHOT

When playing to a hole with little green between the bunker and the hole, the secret is to regulate the distance the ball will fly with the length of your follow-through, rather than your backswing. This technique is rarely recommended, but it's the best for playing short sand shots. Make sure to cock your wrists on the backswing and get the clubhead up above your hands. Hold the clubface open as you finish, and resist like crazy. Remember: short follow-through for short shots. Some players grip more tightly with their left hand to help them accomplish this goal. You can try this and see if it works for you. I'm certain you will be amazed at how well it works.

Tailoring the Tip

Here's an alternative method that I call the "under-release." By this I mean you release the right hand under the left and keep the clubface wide open. It allows you to send the ball flying high over the lip very quickly. If you cannot relate to the right-hand-under sensation, just think of this phrase: "Keep the knuckles of the left hand up through impact."

Chapter 9
PRACTICE TIP

Many mid-level golfers have good wedge swings, but lose strokes due to bad distance control. If you have this problem, here's a drill that will help you learn to hit the ball close with wedges.

When practicing wedges, lay out several balls on the ground, located 15, 20, 25, 30, and 35 yards from the green. Starting 35 yards away, work your way through all of the balls. This drill will enhance your distance control—big time!

To get even better, lay down some more balls and change your target a few times. You can even change wedges. I think you can understand why tour professionals like Len Mattiace, who works on this drill, are such good wedge players.

Laying balls out at different distances *(left)*, then going through each pile hitting to a specific target, such as a towel set down in the grass *(below)*, is a great wedge-practice drill. It gets even better when you hit more balls and keep changing targets.

WEDGE–PLAY INSTRUCTIONS FOR ADVANCED GOLFERS

Chapter 1

DISTANCE-CONTROL PITCHING TIPS

Controlling how far the ball carries or flies in the air, then bounces and rolls comes under the popular umbrella of what pros like Tiger Woods call "distance control."

If you think back to the time you graduated to Advanced status, you will recall how the game became suddenly much more controlled. The game became more precise, and the reason is that when you become a low-handicap player, you must know how to control your ball flight to hit shots closer to the hole and make those all-important birdie conversions. When you do that on a steady basis, you take your game to the next level and play pro-standard golf—albeit probably not as consistently as the tour pros.

Here are some vital distance-control tips to get you started.

CONTROLLING DISTANCE WHEN PLAYING DOWNWIND

When hitting a shot with a strong wind at your back, don't do what the majority of advanced players do: take one or two clubs less than normal—i.e., a lob wedge instead of a pitching wedge and launch the ball high into the air. I know I'm surprising you here, because most of your golf partners will tell you to do this. The fact is your friends have not been as fortunate to converse with the game's legends and learn their secrets.

The consensus among golfing greats is that taking less club makes it even more difficult to control the shot. The advice given to me by such great Texas wind players as Tom Kite and Ben Crenshaw is to take the club for the distance at hand, but to do a few things differently. Position the ball farther back in the stance, make a controlled three-quarter swing, and play a controlled punch shot by hitting down and through the ball. Now the ball will fly at a low trajectory under the wind and not carry farther than expected. Instead, it will "hunt the hole," to borrow a line from golf commentator Gary Koch, a terrific wind player in his own right. This shot makes distance control for the downwind shot significantly easier.

CONTROLLING DISTANCE BY KNOWING WHEN TO CHOOSE THE STRONGER CLUB

During a round of golf, you will often assess your yardage and conclude that you are halfway between clubs. You don't know whether to hit a hard sand wedge or an easy gap wedge. In such situations, I advise my Advanced students to go with the longer and stronger club.

It's much simpler to make a nice controlled swing with the stronger club (the gap wedge, in the case just cited) than to choose the weaker club and have to swing out of your shoes just to reach the hole. Furthermore, you will maintain more consistent tempo, timing, and rhythm by selecting the stronger club, whereas swinging the weaker club hard will only lead to a loss of balance and a bad shot.

Chapter 2

THE PART-SHOT WEDGE

I'm always baffled by golfers who believe that a player who can't get home on a par-five hole should lay up within full-wedge distance rather than part-wedge distance, because they claim it's easier to hit a full shot than a part- or half-shot. Often this is simply not the case. Unless the pin is tucked very near a bunker or lake, or the green is rock hard, getting closer will always increase your chances of hitting a better approach shot.

Based on my own game and that of other PGA Tour pros, as well as advanced players I teach and play with, I know that almost anyone can learn how to put plenty of backspin on the ball with the half wedge from, say, forty to fifty yards. Therefore, I think it might be bad advice to suggest that it's smart golf to leave the ball one hundred yards or more from the hole when you have the chance to put it within half that distance. I've heard all the arguments about how much easier it is to hit the ball closer to the hole with a full swing as opposed to a part- or half-swing. The logic being that it is easier to judge a full swing and how far the shot is going to travel. I disagree with this reasoning. All true short-game artists will confirm that it's easier to control a shorter shot and attack most pin placements. Heed the following instructions for playing the part-shot wedge with a sand wedge or lob wedge.

Play the ball near the center in a narrow, open stance. Distribute your weight evenly instead of favoring the left foot as you would most often do on wedge shots. This adjustment plus swinging on a slightly flatter rather than steeper plane will allow you to hit a sweeping type of shot and take a shallow divot—a mere scrape, in fact. This more sweeping action will also help give the shot more immediate height and stopping power, as opposed to the more downward blow used for the full wedge. Before swinging back, focus hard on your target, since reading distance with your eyes relays a message to your body on how big a swing to make.

Practice will also tell you exactly how far to swing back. However, you will never need to make a full swing from just a short distance. By the same token, you don't want to employ too short a swing either. Again, develop feel through practice.

On the downswing, concentrate on working your right knee and swinging the club briskly through the impact zone and out toward the target. Brushing your chin against your right shoulder as you swing through will encourage good acceleration.

When you practice these shots, carefully pace off your 40-, 50-, and 60-yard distances. Use a 10-yard gap as you hit shots alternately to each distance marker.

Chapter 3

THE KEN VENTURI TURN–RIGHT WEDGE SPINNER

Whenever the hole is situated directly behind a sand bunker or water hazard guarding the right side of the putting surface, there's an alternative strategy to going straight for the flag.

At address, play the ball up in an open stance and aim left of the hole, toward the "fat" part of the green. Set the blade of your pitching wedge open. Position your hands well forward of the ball.

Swing the club back outside the target line but parallel to your hip line, which was set left at address.

On the downswing, get the sense of pulling the club across the line with your left hand. As you go through the impact zone, "hold off" your hand release. Keep the knuckles of your left hand up all the way to the finish.

This setup and swing will allow you to hit a shot that curves to the right in the air, lands on your target left of the flag, bounces right, and spins right toward the hole.

Chapter 4

DRAW–SPIN WEDGE LESSONS

This is the formula for playing a high-percentage right-to-left shot when the hole is tucked behind trouble on the left side of the green or when the green slopes severely.

Play the ball farther back in your stance than you normally would when hitting a standard wedge shot, and aim right of the hole, to the fat part of the green. Set up with your shoulders, hips, and feet closed, then take the club way to the inside on a flatter plane. The key to this shot is how you release the forearms going through

Swing down from the inside. When entering the impact zone, rotate your right forearm counterclockwise to close the clubface slightly and impart gentle hook-spin on the ball so that it turns left toward the hole. The ball will hit the green and spin left toward the hole. This is a great scoring shot that can allow you to attack many back-left hole locations.

Chapter 5

NINETY-YARD DEAD-BALL SHOT TECHNIQUE

Here's a true "scoring weapon" shot that all better players need to have when the hole is set deep on the green or is up on a top tier and you're ninety yards away. A full sand wedge is the wrong choice, because of backspin. Chances are your full sand wedge will come in near the flagstick, but check and spin back dramatically away from the hole. Too many times I've seen a player hit a beautiful shot that lands near the pin but spins back down the slope and ends up thirty feet short. Instead of an easy birdie, he faces a possible three-putt and a bogey.

Other golfers take the aggressive route, sending the ball beyond the flag and trying to spin it back to the hole, but that strategy is extremely dangerous. Just a slight miscalculation sends the ball over the green and into the rough or, worse, down a severe slope. This leaves the golfer with a very nasty recovery shot. If he gets too fancy, he'll leave the ball in the rough short of the green. If he plays it too safe, the ball might end up way past the hole and down the other slope.

The shot to play instead is the low-flying gap-wedge shot. When executed correctly the ball will come in soft, take a couple of hops on the green, and stop dead. There will be no exaggerated spin. Here's how to hit this shot.

First grip down slightly. Second, stand closer to the ball. Third, use a three-quarter swing, back and through. Fourth, be sure to stay patient on your backswing. Fifth, pace your swing with body rotation.

These keys will allow you to hit a lower shot, but the real secret to success is quiet hands. The great shot-maker Ken Venturi showed me the dead-hands concept that produces the dead-ball shot. Ken learned it from Ben Hogan and Byron Nelson. Quiet hands are a huge aspect of this scoring shot. You should feel as though your entire right side (right hand, right arm, right shoulder, right hip) is moving together through the ball and to the finish. Never stop the body and flip the hands. Instead, move briskly through to your finish position, with everything working together. Your shots will have much less spin and you'll be able to attack those back pin locations.

Venturi has shown this shot to many top tour players like Tom Weskopf, Tom Watson, and John Cook, to name just a few.

When playing Ken Venturi's dead-ball wedge shot, feel like your hands stay quiet as you come into impact *(above)* and you move your entire right side (right hand, right arm, right shoulder, right hip) all together through the ball and into the finish *(right)*.

Chapter 6

THE JOHNNY REVOLTA SHORT PITCH FROM LIGHT ROUGH

It's very hard, no matter how talented a player you are, to put spin on a ball that is nestled down in the Bermuda grass rough near the green that is common on courses in the southern United States, particularly Florida. However, if you take your sand wedge and follow the instructions given to me by short-game legend Johnny Revolta, you can get the ball from Bermuda grass to sit down on the putting surface quite quickly.

Address the ball with your feet, knees, hips, and shoulders aligned left of the target line, open the clubface, and put sixty percent of your weight on your left foot to encourage an upright swing arc and sharp downward hit.

On the backswing, direct the club back and up sharply along your bodyline, which encourages a slight cut-swing.

When coming down, pull the club down hard with your left arm and hand, concentrating on employing a short finish.

The ball will pop up into the air and land softly.

If you want the ball to pop out of Bermuda grass rough by the green, open your stance and clubface at address *(above, left)*, direct the club up sharply *(above, right)*, and pull the club down and through impact with your left arm and hand, while striving for a short finish *(right)*. That's what short game ace Johnny Revolta taught his students.

Chapter 7

GRASS BUNKER RECOVERY PITCH

Some new golf courses feature grass bunkers around the green, so you'd better be prepared, particularly if the ball is sitting down snugly and you have a limited amount of green to work with.

When setting up to play this shot, take an exaggerated open stance to promote an out-to-in swing and, ultimately, a soft ball flight. Also, open the face of your sand wedge or lob wedge and play the ball opposite your left heel.

Use a compact, upright swing by allowing your right wrist to hinge very early in the backswing.

Swing the club down sharply into a spot just behind the ball, as you would in the sand. However, because you fully release the hands you will not dig deeply. The clubhead will slip under the ball. This explosion-type technique will cause the ball to pop into the air, rise quickly, and land softly.

Chapter 8

LOB-WEDGE CHIP TECHNIQUE

From studying experienced players in the 1–3 handicap range versus those in the 4–9 handicap range, I've noticed that lower handicap golfers hit most of their chips with a lob wedge instead of using a variety of clubs. To improve your play in your own Advanced category, or to get down to scratch, I'd consider the following strategy that is used by many tour professionals.

When playing short chips, these players position the ball just behind their left heel, set the angle of the wrist on the backswing, hold the angle through impact, and slide the clubface under the ball so that it floats in the air and lands softly.

On medium-length and long chips, they move the ball back accordingly (farther on long chips) and use a dead-wristed stroke to hit a low, running shot.

This simple system of chipping is used most of the time by many tour professionals. They prefer this way of chipping because they find it easier to master one club rather than several, and easier to control distance with a high-lofted club.

My suggestion: Take a few balls down to

There's no better way to perfect the lob wedge chip than to hit practice shots—just like the top pros do.

the practice area and work with your lob wedge, hitting different chips. It will take a serious commitment, but I know you'll become very confident and well-versed in it over a period of time. If you play tournament golf or play on hard, fast greens, this technique can lower your scores.

Chapter 9

THE OPEN-FACE BURIED BLAST

When you miss the green with an approach shot and land in a bunker, sometimes you get unlucky and end up with a buried lie. The situation is even more difficult when you "short side" yourself and there is only a limited amount of green between you and the pin. Most of the time you would just like to take your medicine, land the ball anywhere on the putting surface, and get out of there. However, relax. The advanced shot I am going to discuss here will help you get the ball up and in more often from this very difficult lie, provided you sacrifice some play time for practice time.

I usually teach a student to handle a buried lie by using a square or slightly closed clubface so that the club will dig the ball out. For this shot you actually want to do the opposite. Your setup will be similar to a standard bunker shot: a shoulder-width stance and your weight set slightly to the left leg. Play the ball about two inches back from where you would normally play a bunker shot. This will be close to the center of your stance. Before you grip the club, make sure to open the clubface so it looks as if you will hit the ball straight up into the air. Your grip pressure will be 6 or 7 on my scale of 1–10.

Hinge the club up very soon using your wrists during the backswing, with no shifting of weight in order to ensure a sharp descending blow. This shot requires a lot of speed since the ball is under the sand, so you need almost a full backswing. You must hit about two inches behind the ball to get the clubhead under it with an open clubface. Your finish should be very short. In fact, you want to feel as if you've left the clubhead in the sand after impact. The ball will pop out of the sand and land softly on the green.

This shot is not good in wet conditions, yet it is extremely effective on hard, fast greens. Since the clubface is open and is passing from under the ball, the shot will fly higher and land softer with less roll. When using a closed clubface, the ball is squeezed between the sand and the clubface and will almost always come out hot with some topspin. On fast greens, the ball could roll twenty or more feet farther. Again, this shot requires a lot of practice. You should see and know how the ball reacts before you try this shot during the heat of competition. Once you do, this could be a round saver or a match-winning weapon. Your golf partners and opponents won't believe their eyes when they see you pull off a phenomenal shot from such an awful lie.

Chapter 10

SUPER-LONG BUNKER-SHOT SECRETS

The very long bunker shot does not have to be "the toughest shot in golf" if you follow these instructions.

Set up with your feet square or even aiming right, to open up a clear passageway for you to swing the club on a flatter path with your arms and hands.

In playing a long bunker shot, concentrate on swinging through fully and making a total release with your hands and arms.

Take a gap wedge or a pitching wedge, open the clubface and hold it above the sand about one inch behind the ball.

Swing the club back fully and keep wrist action to a minimum. Swing down, making a total release with your hands and arms, striking the sand one inch behind the ball. This action will create more speed, which is essential for this shot. The ball will roll a little more than normal, so allow for this when picking your landing spot.

The best long bunker player I know is Tom Kite. We practiced together many times and I often watched him play in tour events. Besides devoting a good deal of time to practice, Tom focuses on a full finish and a total commitment to the shot. Tom always takes a thin cut of sand and finishes fully over on his left side. It's like he's hitting a five-iron shot, but his contact point is slightly behind the ball.

Chapter 11

EXPERIMENTAL PRACTICE

The one element of the advanced player's game that most often prevents him from attaining his goal of becoming a scratch player is being too set in his ways. Granted, this type of player will make equipment changes every once in a while—trying a new driver, wedge set, or putter, and occasionally attending a golf school or taking a private lesson to improve his golf swing. But in the realm of shot-making, the average advanced player does very little to expand his shot-making game, particularly with regard to wedge play.

The solution to this problem is to be more imaginative about your practice. By all means, practice hitting drives and working on your putting stroke, but also devote more hours to learning new wedge shots (see page seven of color insert in the Wedge Wisdom segment for the Advanced Player) by doing some experimenting.

Becoming a wedge-game virtuoso who can look at a lie and read it—and know exactly whether the pitching wedge, gap wedge, sand wedge, or lob wedge will work best—is vitally important. And by spending some time in practice trying various techniques, you will develop an array of shots. Whatever lie you face on the course, you'll have different shot-making options. Tiger Woods, Lee Trevino, Phil Mickelson, Brad Faxon, Sergio Garcia, Tom Watson, and Seve Ballesteros have all proved that the more shots you have at your fingertips, the better your short game and scores will be even without your "A" long game.

Practicing a variety of short game shots *(opposite)* will make you a more creative wedge game player, as will working the hands differently, such as practicing a right-hand-under move vital to hitting a super lofted shot *(left)*.

What you have to do, then, is to vary your setup and the length of your swing, align the clubface square, open, or closed, and use the different wedges in your bag to hit shots from various lies.

You should practice all types of fun and crazy shots to see what is possible, and to train your hands to act differently. It's fantastic practice to learn clubface control. This is the type of practice young junior golfers do all the time and is a big reason they improve at golf so fast.

A great short-game player has tremendous imagination and great feel. No two shots around the green are exactly the same. That means you need to be creative. If you take the time to practice the small shots, you'll gain a huge advantage in the game of golf.

PART III

PUTTING LESSONS

Putting is an art, not a science, although many golfers don't consider this to be true. A great number of amateurs and numerous pros believe that you must mechanically train yourself to take the putter perfectly straight back and straight through. They also believe you should keep your eyes directly over the ball-hole target line and practice until you become a perfect putter.

This is not what I've witnessed in a lifetime of playing and teaching. Quite the contrary, most good putters, whether on the PGA Tour or on the amateur golf circuit, do not have their eyes on the target line and do not move the putterhead precisely straight back and straight through. Why not?

Well, first of all, it is not a natural human motion. Your arms and hands have to be trained to move in a straight line. It can be done, but it is not a natural movement. Prove it to yourself right now by clapping your hands together. Just watch what your hands do and how they move. To make it more like golf, put yourself into your putting posture, allowing your arms to hang any which way you choose, and again clap your hands. This will show you natural motion.

Next, go up to a wall and again assume your putting posture. Place your hands against the wall, with your palms together in a "prayer mode." Now make your hands slide back and through on the wall. When you do this, allow zero rotation of your palms. That's straight back and straight through, and it probably feels awful. Yet this is the dominant idea today in teaching putting to amateur golfers.

The second major reason for not trying to manipulate the club straight back and straight through, precisely along the target line, is that the minimum lie angle of any putter-shaft is ten degrees—not straight up and down. If you were allowed to straddle the line and putt between your legs in a croquet fashion, a straight-back, straight-through stroke would be easy to employ and work nicely. The United States Golf Association outlawed this form of putting in the late 1960s, when several PGA Tour players adopted the style and won with it. What it boils down to is that you will find it extremely difficult to consistently repeat the motion unless you are willing to spend huge chunks of time practicing.

Let's be brutally honest. I know you understand that any scientific approach to putting is impossibly flawed because you probably know somebody who consistently putts great with some very odd stance and a very different stroke. They may cut across the line, pick the putter up on the backstroke, hit slightly down on the ball at impact, or have a very short or very long finish. Yet they seem to defy the norm and putt great year in and year out. I could go on and on, but you get the idea. You know I'm right.

Good putting is not the result of mastering somebody else's idea of one perfect stroke. Rather, players who hole putts do so because of a repetitive stroke combined with excellent green-reading skills and good visualization techniques. Plus they are extremely confident and possess the ability to roll the ball on an intended line. You and I know that the super-confident putter is to be highly feared, no matter how unorthodox his setup and stroke.

The art of putting is a complex and highly individual matter that requires great touch and feel. To be a good putter, you must also be perceptive and imaginative. Three PGA players all proved this en route to winning the Masters—Ben Crenshaw (1984), Tiger Woods (1997), and Mike Weir (2003)—on the Augusta National course featuring extremely fast greens with extraordinarily tricky breaks. Crenshaw ran the tables with his "Little Ben" putter. It was a putting exhibition that stunned the golf world. Jack Burke, Jr., told Ben he should put that putter in a glass case, light candles around it, and sell tickets to see it. Ben has one of the all-time best natural strokes, unencumbered by conscious thought.

Tragically, many fine putters have practiced themselves into mediocrity or worse by becoming highly mechanical and attempting to master the elusive straight-back, straight-through stroke.

In studying great putters, I have noticed many unorthodox nuances in their techniques. Over the years, I have also interviewed many of the greatest putters of all time, including Jack Burke, Jr., Ben Crenshaw, Brad Faxon, Gary Player,

George Archer, and Bob Charles. All of these great "flat stick" players have convinced me even more about the unique and personal aspects of putting.

For example, Faxon and Crenshaw admitted to rarely practicing. In contrast, George Archer claimed he could never have evolved into such a great putter if he did not practice extremely hard. Gary Player said he copied the stroke of fellow South African Bobby Locke. Locke used a closed stance and almost hooked the putt, or at least it looked that way. In any case, Locke's stroke was anything but straight back and straight through. Both Locke and his protégé Player took the putter back inside and never followed through. Each stopped the putter just after impact. Isao Aoki, perhaps the best Japanese player ever (and 2004 Hall of Fame inductee), did the same thing, except that he stood far away from the ball and just lifted the putter up on the backstroke and then chopped down. Aoki's downstroke was even more abrupt than Locke's or Player's; in his case, the putter stopped moving right at impact. Nevertheless, it worked, and it worked well. In fact, all of these players, though different in terms of methodology, drained putt after putt throughout their careers in huge pressure situations. Locke won the British Open four times and Player won nine major championships.

Raymond Floyd used an exaggerated wrist action in his stroke and cut across the ball through impact. If he had ever had his stroke filmed and watched it as he developed, then changed it to something that did not feel as natural to him, we probably would never had heard from him. Instead, he won two Masters, two PGA Championships, and the U.S. Open. And Floyd often used a thirty-eight-inch putter to do it!

Jack Nicklaus adopted a very unusual hunched-over posture. Working with Jack Burke, Jr., Nicklaus used a piston-like, right-sided push-stroke that always produced a solid hit on his putts. Burke, the great player and teacher, like Tommy Armour before him, favored right-side control over left-side control. I'll get more into this subject when I discuss the putting stroke, but for now appreciate this little-known fact:

Nicklaus would also use different strokes from week to week. He was constantly adjusting, upgrading, and changing different aspects of his setup and stroke. This is a concept totally unknown to most amateurs. The fact is, most tour players adjust their putting setup and/or stroke quite often. Here's a list of what the typical PGA Tour player might do from week to week.

Change his grip.

Change his eye position.

Adjust his head position.

Move the ball closer to his body.

Move the ball farther away from his body.

Move the ball up in his stance.

Move the ball back in his stance.

Employ a shorter backstroke.

Employ a longer backstroke.

Shorten the follow-through.

Lengthen the follow-through.

Swing the putter back straighter.

Swing the putter back more inside the target line.

Work on an arc-stroke.

Swing the putter back lower to the ground in the takeaway.

Swing the putter up more quickly in the takeaway.

Lean the shaft forward at address.

Lean the shaft back at address.

Speed up the stroke.

Slow down the stroke.

Read the putt only from behind the ball.

Read the putt only from behind the hole.

Read the putt from both sides of the ball-hole line.

Read the putt from all directions.

Eliminate practice strokes.

Increase practice strokes.

Change his pre-stroke routine.

Change putters.

In practice, or in time off between tournaments, a tour pro might also watch film of great putters with different styles, looking for just one instructional nuance to help him sink more putts. Tiger Woods still does this today. I doubt that any other tour player would ever experiment with the cut stroke used very successfully by PGA Tour pro Billy Mayfair, but you just never know.

You may want to consider copying some of these different strategies and working on off-course practice drills, too, like those that my student Len Mattiace used in training for the World Putting Championship that he won in 1995. Len putted along either a line of string or chalk line stretching from the ball to the hole, something that Champions Tour sensation Craig Stadler has been doing since the early 1980s. We practiced all types of putting drills and Len eventually won that championship and a $250,000 check.

You get better at putting by building a simple stroke that works for you. To do this, you should experiment and carefully study the different styles of great putters. You should practice on your rug at home, hitting the leg of a table or chair. You should work hard on developing a very positive attitude, making yourself believe that putting will be something you *will* master. Your practice sessions on the putting green should also be well thought out. I suggest short, focused sessions where you vary the drills I provide in this section of the book. I define short putting sessions as fifteen-minute segments. Practice one drill for that period of time, then change to another. Putt for no longer than you can focus. Experiment with different drills on the practice green. Find your favorites and the ones that work for you.

I hope I'm making a great case for practicing putting, simply because it's one of the most critical links to good scoring. Regardless of the vital importance of the driver and wedge, the putter is as significant as the bullfighter's sword, simply because it is the club that all golfers depend on to finish the job—stroking the ball across a green and then into the cup. Yes, no matter how good a golfer's driving and wedge-play skills may be, he or she must be able to possess the talent to hit approach putts close to the hole and sink short pressure putts to shoot low scores and win at any level.

Every golfer, pro and amateur alike, can relate to the emotional swings that come on the greens during a round. Putting truly is a game of inches—fractions of inches, micro-inches in fact. As short-game genius and putting wizard Seve Ballesteros once concluded, some days you putt well during your pre-round putting practice and seem to lose your stroke on the course, while other days you miss practice putts then hole almost every putt on the course. Sometimes you hit bad putts that somehow fall into the side door of the cup. Other times you hit good putts that veer away from the hole for what seems like no conceivable reason. A good putt can miss because of the grain in the grass, a spike mark, or a barely visible imperfection in the green.

What's so mind-boggling about putting is that it requires the shortest stroke of all clubs, yet in between so much can go wrong. You must master your mind to master putting. There is so much more to putting than most golfers would believe. Mistakes are often the result of poor green-reading habits, lack of confidence, or anxiety related to the fear of missing a putt that you expect to sink. Worrying about shooting your best score or needing to hole a putt on the last hole to win a match also affects one's nerves.

In this part of *The 3 Scoring Clubs*, I teach Beginner, Mid-Level, and Advanced players to understand one thing: The best defense against poor putting is knowledge. That means, no matter what handicap you play to, you must choose a putter that is aesthetically pleasing to the eyes, feels good in your hands, is well-suited to your height and hand position, and promotes a technically sound roll. You must also learn to read the break and the grain in greens. I'll show you how to do that based on my long experience as a player and teacher, along with insights from the top putters on the PGA Tour.

Of course, you must learn how to groove a good stroke too, one that may be somewhat unique but still repeats itself under pressure and allows you to hole putts. In addition, you must learn to think your way to lower putting scores, to pace putts, to learn the role that the eyes play, to practice the right way for you, and much more. Above all, you must build your confidence level. Nothing is more important than believing one hundred percent in your system and that you can hole every putt. Gary Player, Ben Crenshaw, Bobby Locke, Jack Nicklaus, Bobby Jones, Arnold Palmer, Tom Watson, Chris Riley, Stewart Cink, and Tiger Woods were or are the best in the business.

Depending on your skill level, the more sophisticated and sometimes radical the instruction, and the harder you practice, the faster you'll move up the ladder of improvement and reach the next level. So let's make our way to the practice putting greens and get started on the next lesson.

PUTTING INSTRUCTIONS FOR BEGINNER GOLFERS

Chapter 1

CHOOSING A PUTTER

There are hundreds, if not thousands, of putters on the market. Most models fall into four basic types: center shaft, mallet, blade, and offset center shaft. Each putter is also short, medium, or long in length, heavy or light, flat or upright, and features a rubber or leather grip and slight variations of loft. You should also

Today, the golf market features a bigger array of putters than ever before, like those shown here. When making your selection, be sure to choose one that gives you confidence and a feeling of balance throughout the stroke, and rolls the ball smoothly across the green.

know that some putters are face-balanced, which encourages a more straight-back-and-through method. Many other putters have quarter toe hang (or more) and encourage an arc-stroke.

Tall players I've spoken to or observed usually putt with a more upright putter, particularly if they like to stand close to the ball with their hands high. Shorter players often prefer a flat putter because they feel more comfortable standing farther away from the ball with their arms outstretched. Other golfers choose flat putters because they hold their hands low, like Fuzzy Zoeller, former Masters and U.S. Open winner. Hubert Green, a fantastic putter, used a split-handed grip with a very flat putter and won twenty-two tournaments, including two major championships.

In the category of loft, some golfers prefer a putter with a low degree of loft, between one and three degrees, because they hold the shaft very vertical with no forward press. Golfers such as Champions Tour player Tom Watson prefer a putter with a high degree of loft (around four to five degrees) to compensate for a forward press prior to the stroke or a slight downward strike at impact. Phil Mickelson putted with a flange putter with eight degrees of loft throughout his younger years and was regarded as the best on the greens.

I love one Mickelson story. In the United States Amateur, Phil famously gave his opponent a twenty-foot putt for par. Phil had a six-foot putt for birdie that he knew he would make for the win. His opponent was a bit shaken when Mickelson holed the putt. That's big-time confidence and one of the most intimidating of all strategies in the history of golf.

As you might guess, choosing the right putter takes time and effort. One good approach is trial and error. Your pro can point you in the right direction, but you are the only one who can determine which putter looks the best, feels the best, and works best for you. However, I always test my students to see if the ball is rolling over correctly. Furthermore, all of the teachers at my schools are trained to use high-speed video analysis to monitor any sidespin and the skid patterns of students who come to learn how to putt better.

Whichever putter you select, whether it's a brand-new model picked out of the pro shop window or an old model handed down to you from a parent or sibling, make sure it gives you confidence and a feeling of balance throughout the stroke, and that it rolls the ball smoothly across the green, end over end.

Another design feature that will help you limit your choices and allow you to putt better is the alignment marking. This line, dot, or arrow, usually located on top or on the back of the putterhead, may help you line up better and thus promote putts that roll true on the intended line.

There are lots of variables to consider when choosing a putter. So before you put your hard-earned money down on the counter, wait until you can stroke a few balls on the practice green and are happy with the result.

Chapter 2
THE SHORT-PUTT SETUP

Putting setups vary, and for good reason. Golfers depend on different positions to feel comfortable and see the line better. Having said that, a square address will usually help beginner players putt more consistently. Let's just say it is a very good starting point. Therefore, when addressing the ball, set your feet, knees, hips, and shoulders parallel or square to the target line. In addition, align

When beginners set up to putt, I like them to set their feet, knees, hips, and shoulders parallel to the target line.

the putter's face perpendicular to the hole on straight putts or directly at the apex of the break on curving putts. You may need to set your head in a position that allows you to see your intended line. I often find that this is not with your eyes exactly parallel to the intended line. Jack Nicklaus, a great putter throughout his career, actually set his head behind the ball but directly over the target line, feeling this setup better allowed him to look straight down the line at the hole and become more confident as a result. A golfer must adjust his head and eye-line to a position that allows him to clearly see the target. From the testing done by Carl Welty and me, I know for sure that this is not the same for all players.

Players also use different types of grips—everything from the cross-handed hold to the claw grip. As you begin, I recommend you copy the majority of top golf professionals and amateurs, who use what's called a reverse-overlap grip with the left forefinger covering the fingers of the right hand. To copy this, rest

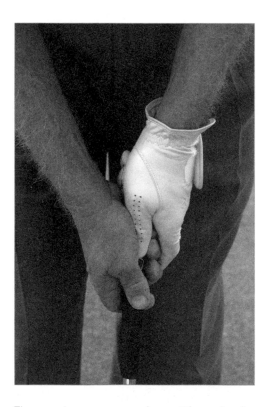 

The popular reverse-overlap putting grip, shown from two angles.

your left forefinger across the first three fingers of your right hand and make sure both thumbs point straight down the putter-shaft. This grip will encourage a uniform connection and serve as a guide as you stroke the ball.

My personal preference is a pendulum-type stroke which can be taught numerous ways. I like beginner students, particularly, to feel that the two arms and the shoulders form a triangle, and that this triangle should stay intact during the entire stroke. So visualize and feel this imaginary triangle at address. I guarantee that the mechanics of your stroke will be better than ever. The real plus factor of this triangle approach is that the stroke will happen more naturally and automatically, without you having to think about mechanics. It will be like putting your car in cruise-control mode.

To complete your setup, play the ball opposite your left heel (more forward if you use a low-lofted putter, farther back if you use a high-lofted putter). Put sixty percent of your weight on your left foot and set your eyes over or just inside the ball or target line. Remember to position your head in a place where you can see the intended line.

Finally, as you set the club down behind the ball so it is aimed directly at your target, the back of your left hand should be square to the putter-face. Think about maintaining this square angle during the stroke and you'll be a much more consistent putter.

TAILORING THE TIP:

I worked with Brad Faxon for about ten years. We spent long hours together, and I watched him play many rounds. Over that time it is unlikely that anyone in the world putted better. Brad is still considered by his fellow players to be one of the best putters on the PGA Tour, if not the best.

One thing "Fax" always does is line up the logo of his golf ball with his intended line. For someone who is super unmechanical, this is something that is technical. Brad is quite careful to precisely aim the logo, which definitely takes practice. It sure works for him, and is something you might try on your short putts. This can be an excellent aid for many golfers. Give it a try and see if it works for you.

Chapter 3

WHAT YOU CAN LEARN FROM THE PUTTING TIPS I GAVE TO SERGIO GARCIA

During the 2003 U.S. Open, I worked with Sergio Garcia on drills to help him improve his putting, which had turned sour over the past year. One major key to his improvement was returning to the natural motion first taught to him by his father, Victor. To dramatically show Sergio how he could improve, I had him putt with a seven-iron. Actually, he just hit mini-chips to various holes. I noticed that he forward-pressed with each chip—moved his hands closer to the target a few inches just prior to starting the stroke. I asked him if he had ever done this with his putting. At this point a bell went off in his head. He realized that he had removed this vital pre-stroke nuance from his putting routine. We put that back, and it made a big difference. The lesson: Go with what has always worked for you in the past.

I also had Sergio change his eye-line, moving it more inside than over the ball. This setup switch allowed him to see the proper line. Apparently, he used to set up this way, but somehow fell out of this good setup. Once he heeded my advice, he played well in the 2003 Open and then finished number one in putting the next week at the Buick Classic at Westchester Country Club in New York. He finished second in that tournament by just one shot.

With a talented player that falls into a putting slump, it is often very help-ful to review past success. I think it is important to recall every possible detail both mechanical and mental. Reviewing past success is certainly one device for quickly regaining confidence.

Most of you will probably putt better with your eyes directly over the ball (as illustrated here), but not all of you! Some of you may find that you putt better with your eyes behind the ball and over the target line like Jack Nicklaus, or slightly inside the target line like Sergio Garcia. In fact, during a lesson I gave Sergio, I had him revert back to his old, natural "inside" eye position.

Chapter 4

THE IMPORTANCE OF A PRE-PUTT GRIP-WAGGLE

I've just discussed the setup and grip types. However, another overlooked piece of top-class putting advice involves grip pressure. Many beginners start with the intention of gripping softly, but as they line up the putter blade, organize their body alignments, and visualize the putt, they unconsciously grip the club more tightly.

You can prevent increased grip pressure by using a grip-waggle. I'm not speaking about a waggle like the one used for a full swing. Rather, I'm talking about merely waggling your fingers and gently "milking" the putter's handle. That means grip, relax, grip, relax, grip again. By actually taking your fingers off the grip momentarily, you tremendously enhance the feel in your hands and you avoid the inevitable increase in tension that occurs when you hold onto the club with no movement. The longer you hold the grip without changing your hand position, the more likely you are to squeeze the putter's handle. I highly recommend that you try this idea of milking the grip with your fingers as you gaze at your target. It is something that I've always noticed Ben Crenshaw do when we played together or when I watched him compete.

Avoid freezing over the putt and locking your hands into one position. Both of these faults can kill a free-flowing stroke.

Chapter 5

THE SHORT-PUTT STROKE AND THE IMPORTANCE OF DOMINATION

I've had great success teaching beginner golfers the idea that one hand and one arm has more control in the putting stroke. This is opposite of trying to time both hands and both arms. It doesn't matter if you prefer to be a left-sided putter like Tom Watson or a right-sided putter like Jack Nicklaus. I've found that focusing on one side of the body helps you set the putter correctly in motion and ultimately roll the ball more consistently along your intended line.

On short putts, this means moving the putter by the domination of either your left or right side, not both. It simplifies your thought process, and it improves the stroke for many golfers. This was another idea I shared with Sergio Garcia. Once he stopped trying to perfect and manipulate the putter straight back and straight through, he started holing more putts. At the 2004 Ryder Cup Matches, Sergio performed wonderfully, sinking putt after putt en route to helping his team beat the Americans.

Something else that helped make Sergio better on his short-putt backstroke was my encouragement that he let his left shoulder rock downward slightly while keeping his head still.

Remember that on a short putt, especially on quick greens, your stroke will be very nearly straight back and straight through. On these types of putts, your hands barely move. Therefore, I believe any exaggerated move that causes the putter to swing inside or outside is detrimental. What you want to employ is a simple back-and-through motion with little or no arc.

From the split second you take the putter back *(top)* to the time you swing through impact *(bottom)*, let one hand and arm (left or right) dominate and control the action.

Chapter 6

THE SEESAW STROKE

Let me explain the concept of a seesaw stroke involving the action of the shoulders, something I stress when teaching beginner students to improve their putting skills.

As you'll see when looking at page three of the color insert, in the Putting Lessons segment for the Beginner player, the left shoulder rocks slightly downward on the backstroke, then slightly upward on the forward stroke. It's important that you create a flat spot in the impact zone, without ever exaggerating it in the follow-through. Again, in putting you're not looking for extra-long club extension through impact. It's okay to hit your putts slightly on the upstroke and slightly high on the ball, provided you are careful not to overdo the upward rock of your forward shoulder.

A short and slow backstroke with a lot of follow-through usually doesn't work too well, although this is precisely what many golfers try to accomplish. It can actually lead to deceleration through impact and poor distance control. Unless a putt is exceptionally long, or the green is extremely slow, the long follow-through indicates a long putt. That long action does not fit with the length of a short putt. So to finish long you necessarily have to go through the putt slow. And again, this often leads to a killer in putting—deceleration.

Believe it or not, the shorter finish action encourages acceleration. Brad Faxon and Len Mattiace, two tour players with whom I have worked, have very distinctive hit-and-hold actions. Lenny tries for an even stoke, meaning the same distance through as he went back.

The next time you watch the pros play in a PGA Tour event, observe their strokes carefully. On short putts, I bet you won't see any kind of hit and drift in any player's follow-through.

A good way to practice this desired action is to stick two tees in the green, not quite as far apart as the length of your putter-face. Next, put a ball down just behind them. Then stroke and hit the tees for resistance, stopping at this point. You'll soon develop the feeling you want, and strike super-solid putts too.

On short putts, solid clubface-to-ball contact is a must, because it decreases the chance of the ball coming up short on a straight putt, or drifting to the low side of the cup on breaking putts. You must contact the back center portion of the ball with the sweet spot of the putter-face to put a good roll on the ball. So work hard on solid contact. Here are some ideas to enhance your practice sessions.

You can use training putters with prongs, or put imprint tape on the putter-face, or simply put some talcum powder on the face so you can tell where you're striking the ball. At our schools, we often recommend that students use a putter with a line on it. Of course, check that line to make sure it is located on the sweet spot. Chi Chi Rodriguez, one of golf's most creative players, dips a ball in water and then strokes putts, making sure the watermark is on the sweet spot of the putter-face to see that he's putting smoothly.

Chapter 7

LONG-PUTTING TIPS

On long putts, it's beneficial to have the clubface of the putter square to the arc of the stroke. Understand, though, that as the stroke gets longer, the putterhead starts moving inside the target line and the clubface appears to open. As you swing into the ball, the putter will come back to the target line and appear to close. In the follow-through, the putter again swings back to the inside. This is natural, just as in the path of your full swing. Your putter is swinging on a plane. Therefore, I usually recommend that you avoid trying to manipulate the club straight back and straight through on long putts. Instead, let the putter swing on an inside-square-inside path.

Just as a repetitive stroke path is essential to good long putting, judging pace is also crucial. Speed control is always crucial on the greens, but even more so on long putts. Acquiring it is just a matter of practicing enough to develop an instinct for the length of stroke you want to make and how hard you want to hit any given putt. Just like tossing a ball or a wad of paper into wastebaskets set at different distances, putting is a matter of feel. To toss the ball different distances, you do not closely monitor the swing of your arm. Rather, you see the target and lob the ball into it. Practice allows you to improve.

Hitting the ball on the intended line is also critical to becoming a good long putter, so it's best to work on drills, such as the one John Daly uses to groove a left-side-lead action that ultimately squares the putter to the ball. Seve Ballesteros has always worked on drills to groove right-side control. (It doesn't matter which way you choose to go, left or right, as long as it simplifies your thinking and helps your putting.)

Daly likes to feel the control of the putter with the lead of the left arm, so he practices this way, knowing that drill-work enhances his timing and direction

If a right-hand- and right-arm-dominated stroke does not work for you, practice hitting long putts with just your left hand, like John Daly.

control. I've watched John hit putts from ten to twenty feet for thirty minutes or more with his left arm only. He puts his right hand in his pocket and practices rolling ball after ball at the cup. If you do this drill fifteen minutes a day for seven days in a row, you will absolutely gain a great feel for the left-side-lead action on long putts. (To hone this same type of action for short putts, practice from four to six feet, letting the back of your left hand drag directly at the target. My old friend Andy North, a two-time U.S. Open champion, would hit thousands of putts with the left arm, and he was always a tremendous short-range putter.)

I've also watched Seve Ballesteros and many other tour pros practice with the right hand only. This type of practice puts the dominant hand and arm in control for right-handed players. I particularly like this idea of your dominant side in control, because I feel it promotes a very natural stroke. Hit long putts in the thirty- to forty-foot range, again for fifteen minutes or more a day for a week straight, and rest assured you will develop a much more free-flowing, fluid stroke. You'll naturally swing the putter on an arc, and in short order learn to hit the ball with the sweet spot of the putter's face. As a result, you'll improve your touch and feel—and your distance control.

My preference here is right-side control for right-handed putters. The reason is that you do everything else in life with your dominant hand and arm, such as starting the car, eating your meals, or throwing a rock. You have more touch, feel, and practice with your dominant hand. That's why most people I teach, though not all, putt better using right-side control.

Chapter 8

READING BREAKS, READING GRAIN

I suggest you take a page out of the green-reading notebook of the pros, who start looking at the slopes or breaks in a green as they approach the putting surface from as far out as one hundred yards. You would be surprised how much a tour professional can detect from this distance. Once on the green, they will quickly analyze the surface and determine how water drains off, which also helps them determine break. They often walk around the side of the green to get a bird's-eye view from behind the cup. On the walk back to the ball, they next look at the putt from both side angles. Finally, they look at the putt from behind the ball and mentally rehearse the ball rolling along a line that they've chosen, before falling into the cup. You should closely observe good putters on tour and adopt the techniques that work best for you. This strategy is truly the shortcut to reaching your goal of becoming a masterful putter.

If you cannot read the correct line, you must consistently mis-hit putts in order to make putts. Don't forget this.

When judging the grain, if the green has a shiny look, the grain is running toward the hole, so you should stroke the ball easier than normal. If the green's surface is dull, the grain is running toward you, a sure sign that you must stroke more firmly to reach the hole.

Let me let you in on a little secret about what I teach advanced golfers. I teach all of these advanced players a slogan for specialty putts that golfers in Florida, in particular, have to deal with. The following two tips, involving 3 **i**'s and 3 **d**'s, will save you strokes when playing in the Sunshine State— guaranteed!

1. **I**nto the grain, **I**nto the slope, and **I**nto the wind equals super-slow.

2. **D**own grain, **D**own a slope, or **D**ownwind equals super-fast.

Finally, great green readers notice every little detail and they do it rather fast. They watch all shots around the green, not only the putts hit by fellow competitors. They have great imagination and always work on their touch and feel.

Chapter 9

PRACTICE TIPS

Golf is a constant learning process, even for players on the Nationwide, PGA, LPGA, and Champions Tours. Therefore, use your practice sessions to try variations on your pre-stroke routine and actual stroke. Let me give you some examples:

1. If you have trouble seeing the line at address, set your eyes behind the ball but along the target line, like Jack Nicklaus. For longer putts, stand taller to the ball, like Ben Crenshaw did en route to winning two Masters tournaments.

2. If your normal stroke does not work well on windy days, practice widening your stance for better balance, bending more from the knees for better leverage, gripping down for added control of the putter-blade, and making a shorter, firmer stroke.

3. If short putts give you trouble, make a drastic change in your grip. Try a double-reverse-overlap grip, cross-hand grip, claw grip, or a split-handed grip. Alternately, try an unorthodox style, such as that used by the 2004 PGA Tour top-thirty player Briny Baird. It appears he putts like we all do when we are practicing on the putting green. In fact, he just steps up to the putt and hits it. The thing is, it seems he never misses this way!

4. If long putts give you trouble, try setting your head and eyes more inside the target line, like tour professional Justin Leonard, because this adjustment will help promote a more natural inside-square-inside stroke. This

Putting like PGA Tour player Briny Baird may solve your short-putt problem.

will help you hit putts more solidly, and that's crucial to improved distance control.

5. If you can't seem to put a pure roll on the ball and get the ball rolling smoothly across the putting surface ASAP, concentrate on hitting the equator of the ball, a tip that putting guru Carl Welty teaches all golfers. This seemingly simple idea is crucial in promoting a great roll with no backspin at all.

6. Check the loft of your putter. Most tour pros use three to four degrees loft. Now, with new groove-face technology—namely C-groove putters or Garon Rite putters—"flatsticks" can have only one degree of loft. The grooves provide lift and thus promote a very quick forward roll on the ball. Retief Goosen has won two U.S. Open championships with a groove-face putter.

PUTTING INSTRUCTIONS FOR MID-LEVEL GOLFERS

Chapter 1

USE THE BELLY PUTTER FOR STROKE IMPROVEMENT

Many mid-level golfers who have trouble with their stroke are often unaware of their problem, and instead try to set their putting game on track by purchasing a new putter. My advice is to not be so quick to blame your putter, although I agree that sometimes a new model can bring you renewed confidence and other times actually help you employ a better stroke. That happens when the new putter is better suited to your needs because it looks good to the eye and features the proper lie, loft, weight, and shaft flex.

In many cases, you can cure the most common stroke problems by using the belly putter. This type of club is especially helpful for golfers who use the hands to manipulate the putter, hinge the wrists on the backstroke, chop down on the ball at impact, or move the head dramatically during the stroke. By practicing with a belly putter for a few hours (see page five of color insert in the Putting Lessons segment for the Mid-Level player), many golfers experience a totally new feel. So ask your local golf professional to lend you one to test on the practice putting green or course.

Champions Tour player and 2004 U.S. Senior Open champion Peter Jacobsen was the first to prove the benefits of practicing with a long putter, claiming that it retrained him to employ a pure arms-shoulders-controlled stroke. I know of several other tour players who practice with a belly putter and then go back to their regular putter for tournament golf. Try this approach the next time your stroke goes sour, then return to your old putter, unless of course you hole so many putts with the belly putter that you feel compelled to buy one. Vijay Singh used a belly putter very successfully for over two years before he returned to a normal-length putter.

You'll find that the belly putter demands a pendulum stroke. By practicing enough, you will likely be able to transfer this feel back to your normal putter.

Chapter 2

HANDLING SUPER-FAST GREENS

Whatever part of the country you play golf in, you are bound to run into extreme conditions on the greens—particularly very fast greens, because so many courses today try to model their putting surfaces after the ones on the PGA Tour. You can also run into this situation when greens are baked out by the sun or the wind, so be prepared. Here's how to handle this situation.

You can:

1. Shorten your stroke and maintain your normal tempo. I like to teach students a very short but smooth backstroke.

2. Maintain your normal-length stroke and swing at a slower pace.

3. Swing at your normal pace and use the same length stroke for the distance at hand, but address the ball closer to the toe-end of the putter and hit the ball with this part of the putter-face. This adjustment deadens the hit and prevents you from stabbing putts on super-fast greens.

4. Visualize the hole several feet in front of where it is actually located. Then try to putt into the imaginary hole. This is a great tip for fast-green putting.

Chapter 3

HANDLING SLOW GREENS

Once in a while the greens at your club will be surprisingly slow due to rain or other extreme conditions. Sometimes, for example, the course superintendent may either be unable or afraid to cut them down for fear of burning them out in the hot summer sun. These are good reasons for you to be prepared to handle slow green conditions.

To putt super-slow greens, you can:

1. Putt with a heavier putter.

2. Make a longer, more accelerating putting stroke.

3. Add wrist action, especially during your backstroke.

Chapter 4

UNIQUE STRATEGIES FOR HANDLING BREAKING PUTTS

Some mid-level players are very good with straight putts into the hole, but really struggle when faced with a sharp breaking putt. Most of the time they under-read the putt and miss on the low, or "amateur" side. If this is your problem, I'd like you to try an approach devised by former Masters and U.S. Open champion Johnny Miller and passed on to me years ago.

When facing a left-to-right breaking putt, play the ball opposite your left heel. This forward ball position encourages the face of the putter to contact the ball as it's almost closing. Consequently, you'll keep the ball left or on the "high side" of the hole and give yourself the best chance of holing out.

When facing a putt that breaks sharply from right to left, play the ball back in your stance and possibly all the way back off your right heel. This position encourages the putter-face to be slightly open at impact, ensuring that the ball will stay right of the hole, once again

This left-to-right putt will stay on the high side of the hole and have a good chance of dropping into it because I played the ball opposite my left heel.

on the high side, where it has a chance of dropping into the side door of the cup or curving into the front door.

Another strategy is to more closely analyze your misses. Many mid-level players under-read the break in a green. I've found this to be especially true on left-to-right putts for the right-handed golfer. To counter this problem, study breaking putts more closely and add more break than you've calculated. Some golfers will need to double whatever they figured, relative to the degree of break. Experiment with this idea until you get the majority of your breaking putts coming in from the high side of the hole, also commonly referred to as the "pro side."

Chapter 5
PUTTING FAULTS AND FIXES

PROBLEM ONE: SWAYING

Mid-level players often are guilty of a very common fault. They move off the ball with a sway, or lean forward and out of their posture coming through the putt. As a result, they putt inconsistently. In contrast, the best putters on the PGA Tour, like Tiger Woods, Brad Faxon, and Jim Furyk, keep their head rock steady.

If you sway and lack consistency on putts, brace your legs to keep them absolutely dead still. I tell students to "freeze the knees," a good buzz phrase that will work for you, too. Alternatively, to achieve steadiness, use the pigeon-toed stance that Arnold Palmer popularized in the 1960s. This setup will allow you to remain very steady over the ball during the stroke and return the club square to the ball at impact.

To really ensure that you cure your sway problem, work on this drill:

Place your head against a post or wall. You can do this with or without a putter. Move your arms and shoulders back and through, all the while keeping your head "glued" to the wall.

PROBLEM TWO: BODY TENSION

If you're a player who gets tense over the ball, makes a stiff-armed stroke, and never knows how you're going to hit the putt (usually either well short or well long of the hole), hold the putter-face slightly off the ground, like Champions Tour player Larry Nelson. You'll see right away how this adjustment relaxes the muscles and makes for a more fluid putting stroke.

PROBLEM THREE: HINGING THE WRISTS

If you are an inconsistent putter because you over-hinge your wrists on the backstroke—so much so that you lift the putter up on a steep angle—take this advice from my old friend Ken Venturi: "Pretend your wrists are in a cast."

This mental image will allow you to make a pure arms-and-shoulders stroke while keeping the wrists out of the action.

PROBLEM FOUR: NERVES

If you shake over a three-foot pressure putt, commonly known as a "knee-knocker," follow the example of Fuzzy Zoeller. While analyzing the line before you set up to putt, whistle like Fuzzy does to relax your nerves. This is a mental trick to take your mind off the result. You can also quietly hum a pleasing tune to better promote good tempo in your stroke.

Another common mistake that causes more nerves and more missed putts is taking so much time over the ball that you think too much. Phil Mickelson improved his short putting by using the following drill given to him by Jack Burke, Jr.

Drill: Put a circle of ten balls around the cup, in the three-foot range. The idea is to sink the first putt and then move quickly to address the next ball, always trying to hole out. When you miss, you have to start the routine over. Jackie asked Phil if he could make a hundred in a row, something that Jackie himself tried to accomplish each evening when he was playing on tour. Phil said it would be no problem, and they bet dinner at the finest restaurant in Houston. Phil made thirty-four in a row before missing. He spent the rest of that afternoon on the putting green at the prestigious Champions course trying for that hundred out of a hundred score. It's a lot tougher than you think. Give it a try.

Phil got so good at holing those putts that he incorporated a version of this drill into his on-course pre-stroke routine and used it to win the 2004 Masters. When facing a short putt, he moves to the side, away from the ball, and makes a practice stroke as if he is doing the drill and has just holed the putt. Next, he simply addresses the ball in play more quickly than he used to, like he does in the drill, and strokes the ball. As you can see from his winning record, this part of his routine has really helped him become a great short putter.

One other pressure tip is to count out numbers as you precisely go through your routine. Once again, it's a mental trick to get your mind in the present tense and out of the future. You do not want to get ahead of yourself and into results. Stay in the moment and with the process.

PROBLEM FIVE: PUSHING PUTTS

Players who push putts often do so because they set their hands well ahead of the ball. Have a friend or your local golf professional check your hand position at address. When you position your hands well forward of the ball, you force the face of the putter to point right of the target, exactly the direction that the ball rolls.

PROBLEM SIX: PULLING PUTTS

Players who pull putts often do so because they set their hands behind the ball at address, which causes you to close the clubface. Have a fellow golfer check your hand position or watch a video of you putting. When you position your hands too far behind the ball, the putter-face will aim left.

Another huge reason for pulling the ball is a mis-hit off the heel of the putter. Make sure to check your contact point if your misses are often left of the hole.

PROBLEM SEVEN: NO CONFIDENCE

To regain a positive mind-set, practice hitting short putts to tees placed in the green. As you begin to hit the tee, gradually move back. The tee, being aboveground, will take your mind off the hole, thereby allowing you to make a more

Practicing putting to a tee will help your confidence when you get to the course, simply because the hole will suddenly look huge.

relaxed stroke. The more times you hit tees in a row the stronger you will become mentally, so that when you return to the course the hole will look huge.

We have our golf school students hit putts at a can of soda set out on the green. Next, we place the can in a golf cup to show them how much bigger the hole is. We then have them hit putts at the hole imagining that the can is in it. This drill seems to help them improve rapidly and really boosts their confidence.

PROBLEM EIGHT: FAILING TO HIT SOLID PUTTS

Believe it or not, your problem might have to do with your equipment. Either the sweet spot on your putter is mismarked or your putter lacks a mark, so you assume the sweet spot is in the center of the putter-face. This is not always true. Here's how to locate the true sweet spot.

Hold your putter vertically above and in front of you by the handle (suspended with just your thumb and forefinger), so the putterhead is at eye level and you can swing it freely. Take a coin in your other hand and tap the putter's face. If the putterhead twists at all, you haven't hit the exact center of percussion. When the putterhead rebounds straight back, you have. More often than not, the sweet spot will be slightly toward the heel of the putter face.

PROBLEM NINE: POOR DISTANCE CONTROL ON LONG PUTTS

Try to get a feel for distance by eyeing the line from the ball to the cup. I want you to really stare at the total target line, from the ball to the hole. Count out the number of seconds it will take for each putt to reach the hole. This process is called "real-time visualization." It is a good exercise that can help your distance control.

This is something I learned from Dr. Craig Farnsworth, an eye specialist and expert short-game coach who taught at my schools for three years. This visual tracking process will help you gauge distance better and pace the ball at a speed that will let it die in or near the hole.

PROBLEM TEN: POOR DIRECTION CONTROL ON SHORT PUTTS

When addressing a putt, align the logo on the ball straight down the ball-hole line or along the line on which you want the ball to start rolling. Brad Faxon and Tiger Woods use this strategy and have proven that it works very well.

Chapter 6

MIND-GAME TIPS

One of the biggest differences between you and the advanced player is the degree to which you use your mind to aid your putting. Ironically, this is an area of golf that gets too little attention. I've worked quite extensively with many top mental experts in golf, including Bob Rotella, Richard Coop, Chuck Hogan, and psychologist Dr. Fran Pirozzolo. Let me share with you some of the best ideas I've learned, so that the power of the mind can help your putting scores.

Tip 1: Visualize a laser-line or ditch running to the hole from the center of the putter-face, so that you're encouraged to roll the ball along this track.

Tip 2: Look for a spot or discolored area in the cup's lining, then putt to this tiny target. That way, even if you just miss your target, the ball will still fall into the hole.

Tip 3: Use a physical trigger to sharpen your pre-putt routine and engage your brain. For example, pull the Velcro strap open on your glove and take it off to putt, or if you putt with your glove on take the Velcro off and then put it back on. This will signal the beginning of your routine, and your subconscious mind will take over. When that happens, you will make a natural stroke without even thinking about technique.

Tip 4: To overcome extreme nervousness before a big match and promote a relaxed state of mind, tell yourself how lucky you are just to be out playing golf. Make it another day to truly enjoy your round of golf.

Tip 5: Visualize a spot six inches in front of the ball along the target line, knowing that if you hit this spot the ball will usually find the hole.

Tip 6: To calm your nerves when standing over a pressure putt, imagine yourself easily holing putts on the practice putting green. Make it just another putt that you have made hundreds of times before.

Tip 7: If you have trouble knocking putts so far past the hole that you usually three-putt, imagine that there's a steep cliff behind the cup. You don't want the ball to fall over the edge.

Tip 8: If you have great difficulty reading the break in the green, imagine a good golfer putting toward you, and watch how the ball rolls and breaks.

Tip 9: If you consistently hit the ball too hard on downhill putts, imagine a fast running stream of water along the line to the hole. This mental image will encourage you to stroke the ball lightly.

Tip 10: When facing a severe uphill putt, imagine that the hole is a few feet farther away. This mental image will encourage you to stroke the ball more firmly.

Tip 11: Before a big match, practice with just one ball instead of three. This pre-round strategy allows you to simulate the one-trial, one-ball game situation, and thus promotes more intense concentration.

Chapter 7

LONG- AND SHORT-PUTT PRACTICE DRILLS

There is no substitute for practice when trying to improve and move from a Mid-Level to an Advanced player. These two drills, one for long putts and one for short putts, will help you get there faster.

LONG-PUTT DRILL

This drill is designed to help you focus more on distance than the stroke itself.

Take your normal putting address and set the putter-face squarely behind the ball and aimed at the hole, some fifteen to thirty feet away. Next, turn your head and look at the hole. Keep your head in that position and make a smooth stroke. This drill may take some getting used to. However, after practice, you'll improve the pace of your stroke and your feel for distance. It will get you much more target-oriented and less worried about employing a perfect stroke.

SHORT-PUTT DRILL

To encourage an accelerating putting stroke and get in the groove of focusing more on the hole than on the line, follow the examples set by the late legend Gene Sarazen, as well as Lee Trevino and John Daly.

The next time you practice putting, speed up your routine and follow the "Miss It Quick" philosophy advocated by these great players. Take a single practice swing, looking at the hole to feel the distance and strength of stroke. Next, just set the putter behind the ball, take one look at the hole, then stroke the putt.

If you dramatically reduce the amount of time you stand over your short putts, you will eliminate many extraneous swing thoughts and worries. So make up your mind behind the ball. Commit one hundred percent to the faster routine and your chosen line. Take your stance, take one look down the line, and then make your stroke.

PUTTING INSTRUCTIONS FOR ADVANCED GOLFERS

Chapter 1

CUSTOM-FIT PUTTING

What sometimes surprises me about some low-handicap advanced players is how they have not yet caught up with the trend of matching the loft built into the putter-face to their hand position at address and through the impact zone.

Up until about a decade ago, most golfers were not knowledgeable about letting the loft feature of a putter improve the roll of the ball and, ultimately, their putting scores. These days, the situation is much different. PGA Tour professionals pay a lot of attention to loft, and that's why they keep in close contact with club manufacturers and both on-site and off-site custom fitters.

When selecting a putter, go by these general rules regarding loft:

1. If you position your hands well forward of the ball when setting up and thus tend to reduce the effective loft of the putter at impact, you should use a more lofted putter, between four and six degrees.

2. If you set up with the putter-shaft in a perpendicular position, a three- to four-degree putter will work best for you.

3. If you tend to exaggerate the up-swing hit through impact, thus increasing the effective loft of the putter, you should select a putter with a loft of around one or two degrees.

4. Slower greens require more loft because the ball needs to get out of its resting spot and up on top of the green.

5. On extremely hard and fast greens, you can use less loft, because the ball needs hardly any lift to start a pure, end-over-end roll.

Chapter 2

LET YOUR EYES HELP YOU PUTT BETTER

It's amazing the role the eyes can play in improving your putting scores if you'll just let them work for you. As an advanced player, it's important that you know this golf fact. However, because I'm constantly surprised by how many golfers neglect this area of putting, here are some tips to help you let your eyes work wonders for you.

Place a twelve-foot strip of masking tape on the ground. You can do this on a carpet or on the cement floor in your garage. Now stand over the line with your putter on the masking tape. Experiment by moving your eyes inside the line, on the line, and outside the line. Also, tilt your head in different positions and see how this affects your ability to look down the masking-tape line. You'll be shocked to learn how much your setup influences your perception. I adjust students until they see their intended line. Some people do better from an open stance and some from a closed stance. I learned this method of lining up from Carl Welty. It is the single greatest teaching idea I've heard for putting. Nobody else that I have ever read or listened to has mentioned this concept—although Tom Kite used it en route to winning the 1992 U.S. Open championship, after I passed on to him what Welty had taught me. It is also one of the things I showed Sergio Garcia.

Chapter 3

SHOULD YOU PUTT LIKE YOU SWING?

Many, if not most, advanced players sink putts using an inside-square-inside arc-putting stroke. These same players tell me their type of stroke path feels more natural because it matches the one they use in hitting normal golf shots. It's the degree of the arc that might differ, some using a very slight arc, others a more noticeable arc. Bobby Locke, one of the greatest putters ever, used this method in days gone by, and today pros such as Stewart Cink, Jay Haas, Brad Faxon, Ben Crenshaw, Gary Player, and Tiger Woods all putt on an arc. The choice is yours, but at least now you know of an option to the stroke that you've been employing.

This type of arc-stroke is now the focal point of Stan Utley's teaching method. Utley, the newest short-game guru, teaches Haas, Jacobsen, and Darren Clarke, star of the PGA European Tour. Stan teaches a very dramatic inside-to-inside arc, and also likes his students to employ a considerable amount of forearm rotation and shoulder turn.

The arc-stroke often gets the ball rolling more smoothly along the green rather than skidding. There is a natural release action. Usually, it's best to position your head and eyes inside the target line, and then simply let your shoulders rotate clockwise on the backstroke and counterclockwise on the downstroke, rather than rock up and down.

Sometimes, putting with a thin grip, lightening your grip pressure, and relaxing your arms so that they feel like spaghetti (without being limp), will also better enable you to use this arc-type of putting stroke more easily.

The re-emergence of the *arc-stroke*—first popularized during the late 1940s and 1950s when South African Bobby Locke used it to win four British Open championships—has even prompted golf companies to invent new training aids for learning this action. Here, I'm working out on *The Putting Arc*, and you see that the ball is destined to fall into the cup.

Chapter 4

THE ROCK-AND-BLOCK STROKE

As good a case as Stan Utley and others make for the arc-stroke, the rock-and-block type of action deserves attention, too. More importantly, should you feel uncomfortable stroking a putt like you swing, you can give this straight-back, straight-through action a try.

Joe Sindelar, Sr., the father of veteran tour player Joey Sindelar, gave the best description of this stroke by using a visual prop. Sindelar had a golfer set up with the heel of the putter against a block of wood, then had he or she slide the putter back on that heel-track.

Putting guru Dave Pelz, who has an excellent checklist of positions to encourage this method, uses a metal-guide training aid to help golfers feel and groove the straight-back-and-through action that he prefers over the arc-stroke. Pelz's training aid, which is a track-trainer, also includes lines to help the golfer keep the putter-face square throughout the stroke, mainly because he believes that there should be zero rotation of the putter during the back-and-forth action. I personally feel this is too mechanical and takes huge chunks of practice to perfect. Yet it can be done.

Both of these teachers want your eyes to be over the ball-target line, but I really like Joey's father's concept of the seesaw. Obviously, so does Joey. He recently won again on the PGA Tour, at age forty-six.

Chapter 5

WHAT YOU CAN LEARN FROM GREAT "DIE PUTTERS"

Many low-handicap experienced golfers, and pros too, have bought into short-game expert Dave Pelz's seventeen-inch theory of putting. Essentially, what Pelz claims is that when addressing a putt, particularly one from long range, you should focus on a spot seventeen inches behind the hole. Then, when hitting the putt, you should hit it at a speed that would allow the ball to finish seventeen inches by the hole if, of course, it did not fall into the hole. According to Pelz, this is the perfect sink-speed.

To me, this theory might hold water on slower Bermuda grass greens or when putting up an upslope, but on slick surfaces I believe you'll end up facing too many lengthy comeback putts to save par. I prefer having better speed control, so that the ball is always finishing around the hole. This is the best way to virtually eliminate three-putting.

Most tour professionals that I talk to on a regular basis agree that it is usually better to be a "die putter" than a "charge putter." This makes sense, because throughout golf history most of the greatest putters let the ball die into the hole. They roll the ball slowly enough that upon reaching the hole the ball either falls into the cup from any side or gently glides by, coming to rest nearby. Examples of great die putters include Bobby Jones, Bobby Locke, Jack Nicklaus, Billy Casper, Lee Trevino, Ben Crenshaw, Brad Faxon, Ernie Els, Jim Furyk, Retief Goosen, Gary Player, and Len Mattiace.

You should at least consider becoming a touch/feel die putter, especially on putts of over ten feet or on fast greens. You may see many more putts drop into the cup if you adopt this proven putting method. When the ball is rolling near the hole at a slow pace, it can fall in from any side of the hole. I say putt aggressively to the hole, not at a spot beyond it. To support my argument, let me relay a message from Bobby Locke to Gary Player.

"Gary, I want to hit putts that have a chance to drop in from four sides of the cup—front, left, right, and back."

Please don't consider this defensive putting. Sure, you might leave a few putts just short of the cup, but that is no worse than a putt that misses going by the hole. The difference is that the die putter always has the golf ball around the hole. Some days the ball falls in from all sides and the player makes everything. But even on days when they don't fall, you still have very low stress. That's because you're not grinding all day long with tough comeback putts that absolutely drain you mentally and eventually cause you to start missing. When that happens, the rest of your game usually deteriorates, too.

I like students to have one basic goal, and that is to ensure that they two-putt. Eliminate three-putts. Ease your stress level by learning to pace your putts so that they're just rolling around the cup. You'll be amazed by how many fall in when you take your mind off sinking putts and turn your attention to rolling the ball on-line at the perfect speed.

Chapter 6

THE SHORT FOLLOW-THROUGH THEORY AND THE BENEFITS OF ADJUSTING

Ben Crenshaw's backswing was long and smooth, but his action through impact was abrupt, and he held it for a moment as well. This type of stroke, as Crenshaw's teacher Harvey Penick taught him, puts a very tight and positive roll on the ball. By that I mean it rolls end over immediately and seems to hug the grass. This proves a big advantage, because the ball rarely wavers off-line. I think this explains why players such as Jack Nicklaus, Gary Player, Brad Faxon, Stan Utley, Isao Aoki, Billy Casper, Dave Stockton, and Hale Irwin all employ short follow-through actions.

The short follow-through is but one way to putt. It is comparable to hitting a nail into the wall with a hammer. The short follow-through promotes acceleration, just the opposite of what a lot of golfers believe. Just think of the hammer and nail and you'll get the idea.

Bob Toski, one of the all-time great teachers, also putted this way. But, he also had one of the most unique ways to practice the short follow-through stroke. Instead of hitting a ball with his putter, he would hit a shoe (see page eight of color insert, in the Putting Lessons segment for the Advanced player) in his hotel room, in the evenings, during a golf tournament, and he told me other top tour players did the same.

If you try this, and you should, you'll find it takes a pretty good blow to move the shoe just a few inches. You'll also find, though, that once you make contact, the putterhead is stabilized. In short, this is a good way to groove the short follow-through stroke.

See how important it is to be innovative when putting. Jack Burke, Jr., another legendary player and teacher, has always been inventive, and what's more he has always believed in making adjustments. All great putters share this philosophy. This is your lesson not to get stuck in one way of putting. "One man, one thousand strokes," says Burke.

One thing Jackie advocated was versatility with your putting. He would say that good putters were good observers. If you pull the first three putts of the day, then you observe and adjust. You do not continue to pull putts all day long. Jackie would immediately adjust his ball position by moving the ball back. If this didn't work, he might put the ball more forward at address. From day to day and week to week, feel changes. It's perfectly logical to make small adjustments, change putters, or choose a different mental image.

Jackie is a big advocate of the right arm and hand controlling the putting stroke. A great tip he used for Jack Nicklaus was pumping the right forearm back and through like a piston. Another tip was to use the right elbow as a governor on the forward stroke. The idea was to start with the right elbow bent at setup and in close to the body. As you stroke through, allow the right elbow to straighten out. When the right elbow extends straight, the stroke ends.

As good as these tips are, on the short finish and right hand and arm controlled stroke, in golf you should always be subject to change. Again, great players make adjustments all the time, such as bending over more or opening their stance at address, when putting. (See page eight of the color insert, in the Putting Lessons segment for Advanced players.)

Chapter 7

DEALING WITH PRESSURE

Pressure is always going to play a role in whether Player A or Player B wins the match. The player who keeps his cool and manages his putting game in the heat of battle is the one who usually wins. So what follows are some tips to help you take your mind off the actual match or stroke-play competition and encourage you to putt well in the process.

1. Have fun by measuring the approximate distance of each putt you holed and then totaling up the amount of yardage at the end of the round. I started doing this when I was competing in professional golf myself. Like the one-hundred-yard rusher in football, I strove for one hundred feet of putts per day. It's an idea that Len Mattiace uses on the PGA Tour. I taught this to him so he could monitor or track his putting performances.

2. Involve yourself in the process of stroking putts and avoid focusing so much on the result. In fact, be carefree in your approach to putting, like Brad Faxon, and you'll hole more putts. Try less!

3. Have a mental key to focus on, such as *low back and low through*.

4. Replay a good putt you holed in the past under intense pressure, so that you can become more confident over every putt—one vivid memory for each pressure putt is the recipe for success.

Chapter 8

PUTTING CURE-ALLS FOR PRACTICE PURPOSES

Even though you play golf at a high level, there is always room for improvement. One of the sure ways for you to lower your handicap is to analyze your putting faults and work on ways to fix them. To get you started, I'd like to present some common problems that even good putters experience when they enter a slump, along with some sure ways to solve them.

HEAD-DOWN TIP:

One of the most important fundamentals for good putting involves keeping the head steady, and this indoor drill will help you do just that. I know this, based on the success I've had with students at the Jim McLean Golf Schools.

Place a golf ball several inches from the base of your family-room wall. Rest your head against the wall, so that your eyes are over the ball or slightly inside that line. Next, swing the putterhead back and through, keeping the toe-end of the blade very close to the wall. Keep practicing until you get the feel for keeping your head so steady that it serves as a fulcrum for your pendulum-type arms-shoulders putting stroke.

GREEN-READING TIP:

If you have trouble reading greens and miss putts as a result, practice learning the art of plumb-bobbing.

Suspend the putter vertically at arm's length in front of you, holding the top of the grip end with your right thumb and forefinger. Obscure the ball with the lower part of the putter-shaft, then look straight ahead with your dominant eye (shut your other eye). If the shaft now appears to be to the left of the hole, the putt will break from left to right. If the shaft appears to be to the right of the hole, the putt breaks from right to left.

STROKE-ACCELERATION TIP:

On long putts, some players swing the putter back correctly, but push the ball to the right of the hole because they decelerate the putter in the hitting area. Decelerating often causes the putter to arrive at impact in an open position, causing the push. If you believe this could be your problem, correct it by practicing the following drill.

Line up two golf balls a couple of inches apart along a particular line. Next, stroke the back ball, trying to hit the one in front of it. Only if the first ball is struck solidly will the second ball be hit squarely. Practicing this drill about twenty-five times a day for a few days will cure your tentative stroke problem and add acceleration to your action.

SHORT-PUTT TIP:

Sinking short pressure putts is critical to scoring, as you know only too well, so here are two practice drills to help you hone your stroke.

Drill 1: Put a dime or a tee on the practice green and putt to it from three feet away. Stroke about fifty putts, so that when you get to the course the 4.25-inch hole will seem like a bucket.

Drill 2: To help you create a less inside-inside stroke that might work better on short putts, hit putts using the leading edge of a sand wedge. Trust me, the ball will never roll purely and stay on track from the get-go unless you make perfect contact on the equator of the ball. It takes intense concentration and a solid stroking action to make putts with the wedge. Once you can start sinking putt after putt with the wedge, you'll have built a much better stroke.

LONG-PUTT TIP:

If your problem is judging distance on long putts, work on this drill that I learned from eye specialist Dr. Craig Farnsworth.

On the putting green, toss one coin about twenty feet from you, another forty feet, and another fifty feet. Each time after making your toss, stare at the line to the coin and then close your eyes. Next, try to walk to where you think the coin is located. Stop and see how far you are from your "target." When you can walk to your coins, you will know you have improved your eye coordination enough to be able to look over a long putt on the course and hit it the right distance.

Putting with the leading edge of your sand wedge will improve your short-putt stroke, making it a less inside action.

As a matter of interest, Billy Casper, one of the all-time great putters, used to pace off long putts. He knew from practice just how hard to hit a twenty-step or thirty-step putt, which is one reason he holed many putts and won so many golf tournaments during his professional golf career, most notably the Masters and the U.S. Open. One of my college roommates, Bill Rogers, did the same thing. Bill won the British Open and was the number-one-ranked player in the world in 1981. Bill, whose nickname was Buck, also concentrated so hard on the line of putt that he mentally burned a track into the green with his eyes. Now that's what I call imagination. Buck was one of the finest putters ever during his time on the PGA Tour.

ACKNOWLEDGMENTS

Writing *The 3 Scoring Clubs* is something I've wanted to do for a long time, yet I kept putting it off until John Andrisani, the former senior editor of instruction at *GOLF Magazine*, and a coauthor of mine on several books, convinced me to go forward. However, I wouldn't have gotten very far had it not been for my literary agent, Scott Waxman, or my business manager, Joel Paige, who both worked out the publishing arrangements with Gotham Books. This publishing house does excellent work, especially due to the fine support I had on this project from my editor, Brendan Cahill.

I learned a whole lot about the long game and the short game by playing so much competitive golf and practicing hard. However, I also gained huge amounts of knowledge in the areas of driving, wedge play, and putting through my time with great teachers such as Claude Harmon, Sr., Harvey Penick, Johnny Revolta, Carl Welty, and Jack Grout, as well as very talented players, namely Sam Snead, Jack Burke, Jr., Gary Player, George Archer, Lee Trevino, Jack Nicklaus, Bob Charles, Ken Venturi, Tom Kite, Brad Faxon, Bernhard Langer, Gardner Dickinson, Len Mattiace, and Peter Jacobsen. I thank them all.

I'm also thankful for the feedback I continually get from my amateur students, including actor Sly Stallone, a former Beginner player; Mid-Level golfers like Michael Douglas and most of the other golfers I work with at our schools; and Advanced players, namely George Zahringer, Liz Janangelo, Cristie Kerr, and Eric Compton.

As far as putting the book together, I owe gratitude to John Andrisani, who served as the chief editorial consultant and whom I commend for a job well done. I'm also grateful to photographer Peter Barmonde for his photographic work.

I would be remiss if I did not pay tremendous tribute to my great staff of Jim McLean Golf School instructors at the Doral Resort and Spa in Miami, Florida; Weston Hills in Fort Lauderdale, Florida; and La Quinta and PGA West, both in Palm Springs, California. I thank you all for your hard work and creative input.

Last, I thank my family—my parents; wife, Justine; and sons, Matt and Jon—for supporting me.